IN THE MORNING OF TIME

THE STORY OF THE NORSE GOD BALDER

THE STORY OF
THE NORSE GOD BALDER

IN THE MORNING OF TIME

Cynthia King

illustrated by CHARLES MIKOLAYCAK

StarLine Edition

SCHOLASTIC BOOK SERVICES

NEW YORK   TORONTO   LONDON   AUCKLAND   SYDNEY   TOKYO

*I am extremely grateful to Mr. Erik
J. Friis of the American-
Scandinavian Foundation for
permission to use material and
quote from my three prime sources:
Henry Adams Bellows' translation
of The Poetic Edda, Arthur Gilchrist
Brodeur's translation of Snorre
Sturluson's work, The Prose Edda,
and Norse Mythology, by Peter
Andreas Munch, all published
by the American-Scandinavian
Foundation.*

C.K.

A hardcover edition of this book is published by Four Winds
Press, a division of Scholastic Magazines, Inc., and is
available through your local bookstore or directly from Four
Winds Press, 50 West 44th Street, New York, New York 10036.

First printing   September 1973   Printed in the U.S.A.

For JK

and also for GORDON,
AUSTIN and NATHANIEL

CONTENTS

1: BEFORE
THE STORM

Hearing I ask of the holy races,
Old tales I remember of men long ago.

Just outside the eastern gates of hell there is an ancient grave, and damp mists swirl about it. In the morning of time soon after the First War with the Wanes, the Great God Odin, Father-of-All, stood straight and still by the tomb. He listened to the dry, cracked voice of the long-dead wise woman, the Vala, who rose out of the mists and appeared before him.

The Vala said:

> "Much do I know and more can see
> Of the fate of the Gods, the mighty in fight.
> Wise is my speech and my magic wisdom,
> Widely I see over all the worlds.
>
> I see for Balder the bleeding god
> The son of Odin his destiny set.
> Brothers shall fight and fell each other,
> Sisters' sons shall kinship stain.
>
> Hard it is on earth with mighty sinning,
> Axe-time, sword-time, shields are sundered,
> Wind-time, wolf-time, ere the world falls;
> Nor ever shall men each other spare!

The sun turns black, earth sinks in the sea,
The hot stars down from heaven are whirled;
Fierce grows the steam, the life-feeding flame,
Till fire leaps high about heaven itself."

The First God, Odin, listened in silent anguish to the Vala's prediction of Ragnarok, the final destruction of the world. When the dead woman of hell sank back into her grave, Odin started his long journey back to heaven. On the way he stopped by a well and asked the dark elf who closely guarded it permission to look into the murky waters.

The elf was miserly and possessive, and said no. His well contained secrets that could twist men's souls.

Odin said he would give any treasure for a chance to see into the well, because he knew that knowledge of good and evil was stored there. He had created the world and all things in it, Odin told the elf, but he could not preserve it from Ragnarok—doom and destruction—without knowing the sources of evil.

The dark elf was not fond of Odin, and therefore the cost was high. He asked for one of Odin's eyes in return for the right to look into his well.

When Odin returned to Asgard, the home of the Gods, he had but one eye. He had looked into Mimir's well, but he told no one what he had seen.

2: THE FEAST IN VALHALLA

*Eight hundred fighters
through one door fare
When to war with the wolf
they go.*

Most of the Gods came into the great stone dining hall laughing. They passed by the wolf who stood by the western entrance, nodded to the eagle who hovered above this door to Valhalla. Then each god paid his respects to Odin and his wife, the goddess Frigga, before he hung his shield on the wainscoting behind his highbacked chair and took his place. At first no one noticed that Balder, usually the happiest of all, was somber and sad.

Frigga held her shawl of hawk feathers close about her shoulders and kept a careful watch and an attentive ear to the clamor and chatter of the huge company. Now and then she said something to Odin as the Gods and Goddesses and hundreds of heroes came in through the many doors and took their seats for the nightly feast. Before the evening was half over, Frigga tugged on Odin's arm. "Look at Balder," she said. "What is the matter with our son Balder?"

One-eyed Odin looked down the long table to where his second and most perfect son sat. Balder was Frigga's first born and favorite, a beautiful god whose thoughts were the purest, whose soul the most generous, whose features most perfect, whose laughter the clearest. All men loved Balder. On earth he was compared to those perfections in nature that men enjoyed—a midsummer day, the coming of spring, the innocence of children. He was called Balder the Beautiful and Balder the Good, and where he went there was joy and laughter among men and Gods and heroes alike.

Now Odin saw that his son was pale, his eyes hollow and haunted, his once smooth forehead drawn tight in a frown. Balder pressed his hands to his temples as if in pain. The Gods and Goddesses who sat near him were quiet and appeared frightened by what he was saying. Bragi, the wise old bearded poet, who often entertained the crowd at night with stories and songs, stopped talking. Balder's wife, Nanna, whose blue eyes usually shone merrily like dancing sapphires in her pretty round face, now pressed her pale cheek against Balder's shoulder. Her eyes were big and pooled with tears.

Odin frowned and said quietly to Frigga, "Where is Loki? Is he in Asgard tonight?"

"I don't know," Frigga answered, "but I am glad if he is not. That son of a giantess, father of a wolf, taunts and tortures me."

"I feel safer when I know where he is," Odin said.

"When Loki is here, misfortune follows," Frigga argued. "It has always been that way. Loki has brought us nothing but danger. Even his children have menaced us. If only we could keep him out of Asgard forever!"

Odin said rather sharply, "You know very well we cannot do that!" He whispered something to each of the big ravens, Hugin and Munin—Thought and Memory—who sat on his shoulders. Each day he sent these black birds out over the world to gather news, and each night they returned and reported to him. Then the Father-of-All placed both hands on the table and called out so his words resounded the length of the great hall, "Balder, my son!"

Balder rose. "Yes?"

"What troubles do you have?" Odin asked. "Why is your face as white as your clothes? Why are your eyes dark and despairing?"

"I have had dreams, Father," Balder replied in a low voice. The huge hall was suddenly silent.

"What kind of dreams?" Odin asked.

"Baleful dreams," Balder said.

"Come and tell me what you have seen in your sleep," Odin commanded. Balder walked down the length of Valhalla to where Odin sat. Nanna followed close behind.

Valhalla, the great stone dining hall of the Gods, was the largest structure in Asgard. It had five hundred and forty doors and could seat eight hundred heroes. Its roof was of silver shields, and its rafters were spears. Each night Odin, who was Father-of-All, sat at the end of the long dining table with his ravens on his shoulders and his two hungry wolves, Freki and Geri—Greedy and Ravenous—by his side, and presided over the evening feast. Before the meal began, Odin had his servants bring in the swords and place them above the table. They gleamed so brightly there was no need for other light.

Then the Gods and Goddesses, lesser and greater, sons and stepsons, wives and sisters and daughters, gathered with Odin's chosen heroes for the festive and often raucous meal.

The heroes were men who had died bravely in battle, and they always came into Valhalla laughing and jostling each other, talking about their day's duels, how many giants they had killed, what wars among men they had joined, and how many newcomers to Valhalla would arrive that night. Each day Odin's armor-clad messenger women, the valkyries, brought all the dead soldiers from Midgard, the land of men, to Odin's court in Asgard. There Odin and Njord's daughter Freyja, the goddess of love, judged the dead. Freyja, who drove through the sky in a chariot drawn by two cats, took half the fallen heroes to be servants in her home, and Odin took the other half for his company of chosen heroes, soldiers who would protect men and Gods from the giants.

No matter how many fallen heroes arrived each day in Asgard, there were always enough seats for them at the feasting table in Valhalla. Those who had been wounded during the day, either jousting about in the courtyard or engaging in the more serious battles with the giants, were already healed and ready for a night of carousing.

When the Gods and Goddesses and heroes were seated, Odin would clap his hands and call for the valkyries to pass the mead. Mead was a strong drink that flowed everlastingly from a huge crock kept full from the teats of the goat, Heidrun. This goat stood on Valhalla's silver roof and chewed the needles of the overhanging tree. Gnawing on the roots of the tree was a red stag from whose antlers enough water ran to fill twelve rivers in Asgard and thirteen in the world beyond.

Odin would clap his hands again and call for the

meat to be brought around the table. The great boar, Saehrimnir, was boiled every night for the feast, but the next morning he was as alive as ever, ready to be cooked and eaten again. Odin did not drink the mead, nor did he eat. He gave his share of meat to Freki and Geri. Odin drank wine—never mead—with whichever of the Gods he chose to honor.

Normally the heroes downed so much mead they would become noisy, boisterous, and often quite drunk; the Gods would stay late into the night, telling stories, listening to Bragi's histories of great doings in other worlds and old times. But this night was to be different.

As Balder the Good began to tell Odin about his dreams, some of the Gods and Goddesses left their places and gathered in a close, silent circle around him. Odin studied their faces. The mighty giant-killer Thor was worried and tugged at his gloves of strength. Thor's wife, Sif, with her long golden hair, sat close beside him. Lonely old Njord, the gentle god of the sea, came and listened, and so did his bright son Freyr and his beautiful daughter Freyja. One-handed Tyr, Odin's bravest soldier, came to listen, and so did Bragi the poet and many others.

Beside Balder stood his blind brother, Hoder, tilting his head as he always did toward the sound of a voice. Odin looked at these two sons of his. Hoder's face was as dark and craggy as Balder's was smooth and fair. It seemed that for every blessing the fates had given Balder, one had been denied Hoder. There was strength in the blind god's thin face, but no beauty. His mouth was sad, and his skin was sallow. Where Balder could laugh, Hoder was silent. He lived in the shadow of Balder's life, helping Nanna, talking with Forseti, Balder's son, seeing the world only through his brother's eyes. But, Odin thought, where Balder asked questions, Hoder found answers. The All-Father watched Hoder's face as Balder spoke, and saw reflected there the dire events Balder was relating.

"I have had terrible dreams," Balder said, "dreams of evil and fire and dreams of blood, dreams so violent and strange that I could not sleep through them, but neither could I waken until they had run their ghastly course."

Nanna turned to Frigga and explained, "He tossed and twisted and cried out so loudly that I had to shake the sleep from his racked body." She put her hand on Balder's arm as if to soothe him.

"Even after I woke I could not seem to escape the fires that leaped around me," Balder told Odin, "and when I awoke I was soaked in sweat."

" 'Lie softly,' I told him," Nanna explained to the others in her soft and velvety voice. " 'It is only a dream. Wash your face in the cool spring water and breathe the new morning air. Then what you have seen in your dreams will be history, nothing more. Perhaps the mead was too strong,' I said, 'or Saehrimnir's flesh too heavy last night.' "

Balder hushed his wife and continued to talk. "The next night it was the same," he said, "and the next and the next. I do not understand anything that has come into my dreams."

Bragi, the wise old poet, listened to Balder and then tugged at his thick white beard. "Why should Balder have nightmares?" his pretty wife Idun asked him. "What has he done?" Bragi shook his head and murmured in a worried tone, "I do not know."

"How long have you had these dreams?" Odin asked Balder.

"For many more nights than I can count," Balder replied. "In the morning of time when all the worlds were new, men and Gods lived in peace, and I slept like the rocks. I never woke until the wolf chased the sun into the sky. But now it seems there is always strife somewhere, and in my sleep strange creatures come, voices from other worlds. Hardly do I lie down before the howling of wolves and the crying of children echoes in my head."

"There has not been a day without a battle somewhere," the bright god Freyr said, "since the First War with the Wanes." Njord sat up sharply and looked at Odin. Once this most peaceful of Gods had been the chief of the race of Wanes. Odin turned his head away and spoke to Balder again.

"Tell us more," the All-Father said to his most perfect son. "Tell us everything from the beginning. Relate every detail. Omit no memory. Dreams are the coded messages of the fates. No warning is more important than a dream!"

Balder sat down and put his fist to his forehead, closed his eyes and began to speak. The gods came closer and were quiet. As Balder talked, it seemed as though he were in the dream again, and Nanna pressed his arm to her side as if to protect him from the world he was entering.

3: BALDER'S DREAMS

Of old was the age when Ym[...]
*   lived;*
Sea nor cool waves nor sand
*   there were;*
Earth had not been, nor
*   heaven above,*
But a yawning gap and grass[...]
*   nowhere.*

The moon knew not what
*   might was his;*
The stars knew not where
*   their stations were.*

The First Dream—I stood at the door of a shepherd's hut of turf, and the wind blew past my head so hard I knew the tawny eagle giant, Hraesvelgr, who sits at the corner of heaven, was angry and was flapping his wings. I heard an animal howl and a baby cry, and I threw my weight against the door, but it would not open. My shoulder hurt and my white clothes were black where I had pressed against the unforgiving door. The baby cried again, so I called out, "The wolf is chained. There is no need to cry!"

The hut melted as if it were made of snow, and I found myself in a lonely place between two pillars of rock, and a baby—blind as Hoder—was in my arms. Then I saw two men who looked so like each other they could have been reflections, sitting by a fire. Each held a long stick over the flame with something roasting on the end. The strong smell burned my nostrils.

"What are you cooking?" I asked them.

They looked at me, then turned back to their spits without words. I went closer to see. Suddenly the earth opened wide like a jaw with rocks for teeth, and tongues of fire flew up and licked me. The two men laughed, and the meat they cooked dripped fresh blood, and they tasted it. I saw that each of them had a gaping hole in his chest where his heart had been. I pressed the innocent baby to my chest and, forgetting that it was blind, tried to hide its eyes from the grisly sight. The fire was all around me, and when the flames touched the baby's bare legs, he cried out and wrenched himself out of my arms. I reached for him, but it was no baby of man or god who faced me now—it was the son of a wolf, all snarling, with death in its dripping jaws. I put my hands over my own eyes then, and as the flames singed my clothes, I thought, I have held a blind wolf in my arms and set him free upon the world.

"Where did innocence begin and why did it end?" I cried out loud into the flaming night. Then I woke up.

Frigga pulled her hawk feathers close about her shoulders, and shivered.

"That was the first dream," Nanna said softly. "I woke Balder from his nightmare and held his trembling shoulders until he realized that it was only a dream." She paused and looked at Frigga. "Morning came, and he was his own loving, laughing self. That day Balder and Hoder went down to Midgard. On a rocky isle in a pretty lake they found an eiderduck family. Laughing, they told me how they robbed the nest of down while the mother sat placidly by and watched the father teach his young to fly. Hoder and Balder brought me a whole basket of the soft fluff, and I made a pillow so that Balder's head might rest more softly on other nights."

Odin stroked his chin and with deep concern said, "Tell us of your other dreams."

Balder began to speak again, and this time he told a story that the Gods knew well. The great hall was quiet as he talked, for now even the rowdy heroes drinking their mead sensed that this was no ordinary night, and the tales were no ordinary tales of battle.

The Second Dream—I was nowhere, standing on nothing, suspended in time and space, with mist all around me. I could see nothing—no earth, no sky, no stars, no hills, no trees, no men, no Gods—nothing. My right arm was burning, and my left arm was freezing. As dawn came, I knew I was back before the morning of time, when there was nothing in the whole empty universe but fire and ice and a great steaming gap between.

There I hung in the yawning void, alone. Into this vast emptiness came layer on layer of ice from the north, and from the south came tongue after tongue of fire. And where the two met, the fire was cooled and the ice melted and dripped. These melting drops fell into the vapors about me, and a strange and enormous form slowly took shape.

The mist rose and I saw a giant lying in the gap with arms and legs stretched wide. I seemed to be near his armpit, in a chasm of flesh and muscle, and my head did not reach above his chest. *Ymir,* I said to myself. I knew his name, as all of us have always known the name of the first frost giant.

I would have run from Ginnungagap, that steam-

ing place, but my will would not make my limbs work, as if I were held by unseen, unfelt chains. I was caught, I thought forever, beside that mountainous creature from which now a rumbling and grumbling came. From underneath the elbow near me first a leg and then an arm and then the whole form of another giant emerged. Then under Ymir's hand a woman appeared, then a boy and a girl from under his feet. These four went off into the vapors to begin the whole race of evil giants: Frost-giants, hill-giants, fire-giants, and even Hraesvelgr, the wind-giant, are descended from Ymir. All were strong, and none knew the difference between good and evil.

In my dream I put my hand to my mouth and called out to them. "Stop! Wait! Do not go away until you know the power of your own strength. Fire will burn, and ice will freeze, and wind will tear men's hair and hurl stones. Be careful!" But just as my legs had not moved when I wanted to run, so my voice had no substance when I wanted to speak. I was alone again with Ymir in the yawning void, and in the chaos of vapors surrounding us I knew the evil giants were multiplying faster than I could count them. Suddenly the rumbling grew so loud that my body shook with it. Ymir knew my fears and laughed at me. When he laughed, I thought my head would explode with the sound.

Balder paused as if tired, and for a moment no one said anything. Then Freyr, the brightest of the Gods, said, "I've heard Bragi tell the story many times, and we all know that out of Ymir's flesh the world was made, but never have I heard this kind of sense put into it. Did you see the cow in your dreams?"

"Yes," Balder nodded. "Sometimes I was tired,

and the dreams went on for many nights, but it seemed that I had to live through every moment of the creation, and I was never allowed to speak, though questions and warnings crowded my brain, aching for release. Time was slow during those nights, though to tell it now seems quick."

"Go on," Odin said. "Tell us more."

Ymir was hungry, Balder continued, and above my head the melting ice became the cow Audumla. She was so huge that at first I could see neither her head nor her tail, but only the four giant udders from which enough milk ran to nourish the greedy monster.

"Don't feed him," I wanted to say to her. "Why should such a placid creature give sustenance to a breeder of evil?" But Audumla's milk went to Ymir, and her tongue licked the salt blocks above her head.

Before my eyes another giant emerged from the salt lick. He was Buri, and in his eyes was hope and gentleness. In my dream I wondered how I could be watching Buri's birth, for I knew he was the father of the good giant, Borr, who married gentle Bestla, who gave birth to my own father, Odin.

I climbed through the vapors away from the crook of Ymir's elbow and up the leg of the cow until I was level with Buri's shoulder. From there I could see into his great gray eyes, like tunnels of light through the mists.

Again I tried to speak, to say I was not yet born, but no sound came from my throat. I was caught in the memory of the beginning of time, staring through those tunnels to an unknown end.

Buri's son Borr had three sons, and those were not giants, but the first Gods. Their names were Odin,

Vili, and Ve, and they knew good from evil, and they knew they were good. Those three were so small, yet they stood proudly in the misty chaos into which they had been born! Odin was wise. He listened to the sound of the wild wind, and he watched the hot fire leap toward the gap, and he heard the roaring of the melted ice, and he felt the rumblings of Ymir's evil laugh, and he was not afraid.

"Come," Odin said to his small brothers, "we will begin a world that is good."

As I watched, Odin and Vili and Ve slaughtered the giant Ymir. When they let the blood out of his veins, it ran in such wide rivers that every giant of his evil race was drowned, except one giant named Bergelmir. He escaped over the oceans of blood in a boat, carrying one giantess with him. They went to a far-off land.

Then Odin and Vili and Ve took Ymir's body and put it into the steaming gap between fire and ice. His body became the earth, and his blood the sea that encircles the world. They took Ymir's skull and raised it high, and that became the sky. At each of the four corners of his cosmic head they put dark elves, whose names were Nordri, Sudri, Austri, and Vestri—North, South, East, and West. And so Odin, the First God, created order out of chaos with the body and bones of Ymir.

"Oh," said Hermod the messenger, "he has dreamed the story that Bragi has sung to us many times. Sing it now, Bragi, for in the dream some of the poetry is gone."

Odin nodded for Bragi to sing, and Balder paused in his account while the Gods listened to their poet once more.

"Of Ymir's flesh the earth was made,
    And of his blood the sea;
    Crags of his bones, trees of his hair,
    And of his skull the sky.

    Then of his brows the blithe gods made
    Midgard for sons of men,
    And of his bitter-mooded brains
    The melancholy clouds."

Then Balder continued:

Odin took sparks from the fires below and set some in assigned places to light heaven and earth, and some to wander along appointed paths. Having created the world out of Ymir's bones and flesh, and the beautiful land called Midgard out of his eyebrows, Odin and his brothers walked around this fertile place along the beach, where the encircling seas lapped the shore. Wise Odin said those waters would be hard to cross, but they would protect the land from the villains in the worlds beyond. The sons of Borr came upon two slender trees, an ash and an oak, near the strand. Odin shaped them into creatures who looked like himself. He clothed them and named them, and said they would begin a new race of dwellers in this lovely land of rivers and valleys and mountains and fertile plains called Midgard. The man he named Ask, and the woman Embla. Odin gave them spirit and life, Vili wit and feeling, Ve speech, hearing, and sight.

Ask and Embla, the first man and first woman, then stood before Odin who had created them and said things to him that made him wonder. "We are two in a strange new universe. Who will guard us against the elements? Do we have enemies? How do we know the order of things? What is good and what is bad? Who will protect us and guide us through time?"

A cold wind blew off the ocean across the new land, and Odin remembered Bergelmir, the one surviving giant, riding away over the waves. He said to the first man and first woman, "You have nothing to fear. It is the morning of time, and there is only good in Midgard. All of the giants but one are dead, and he is so far beyond the ocean that circles Midgard you will not be bothered by him."

"But we are so small," Embla said to Odin, "we cannot even see beyond those hills."

So Odin, the greatest of Borr's sons, made another world above, and this he called Asgard. There he built a tower from which he could watch over the world he had made for men. He created more Gods and gave them tasks. They made tools for themselves with which they built castles and homes, and they built a bridge between heaven and earth out of a rainbow, and called it Bifrost.

To his son Thor, Odin gave great strength, and to Tyr great courage; to Bragi the art of poetry, and to Frigga, his wife, the cares of motherhood and the power to see what lies underneath the actions of men.

In my dream I saw myself standing before my father, holding out my hand. "What power will you give me?" I asked him voicelessly. He frowned, as if he thought I should have known the answer.

"You will be called Balder the Good," Odin said, "because you are created perfectly in all ways. You are and always will be as innocent as a newborn infant. You will need no other power than your purity. The innocent need no weapons."

"But how will I know what I must do?" I asked him. "You must give me something to do."

Odin said, "I have given you perfect innocence. I cannot give you more. You must only be yourself."

I looked down at my feet, and still I stood in the steaming gap beside the rotting body of the giant Ymir, whom my father had slain to make the world. I recoiled in horror at the maggots squirming and feeding on the stinking, bloodless flesh. I turned to look at the Father-of-All to see if he knew that evil fed on evil, and I saw him turn pale. Then he condemned the maggots to eternal darkness.

"Dwarfs they will become," he said in his booming voice, "and live in unlighted caverns below the rocks. Behind their doors of stone they will take men's shapes, though not men's size, and they will be given breath and life and thought."

I turned from the horrid sight and walked through the mists away from the tunnels of time that were Borr's eyes, until I saw before me the lined plaintive face of my brother. "What did Odin give you?" I asked Hoder.

"The gift of blind compassion," Hoder said. I remembered the dreadful sight of the maggots and wished that I, too, could be blind as well as innocent. "What you know about the world of light, I know about the world of darkness. I can see neither good nor evil, but I can sense many things," Hoder said.

"In the morning of time," I said to him, "there is no evil. The world is too fresh, like spring, and too young to know what lies ahead." But in my walk through the mists I had come to the edge of a new cliff. Below me I saw a wall of fire. Men and dogs were fighting it, beating at the flames with branches and sticks. The dogs barked; some screamed.

I had to stand and look. Hoder beside me said,

4: THE TREE OF LIFE

An ash I know, Yggdrasil its name;
With water white is the great tree wet;
Thence comes the dews that fall in the dales.

When Balder finished telling the second dream, Frigga's face was ashen. "What does it mean?" she said. "What does it mean?"

Bragi spoke softly. "Dreams are like memory-stones, histories of fear."

"But not Balder's dreams," Hoder said angrily, his brow knotted in a taut frown. "Balder's memory cannot have evil images such as these!"

Odin said, "Dreams—like runes—can also be the writing of the fates. We Gods must learn to read what is written."

"What do you mean?" Frigga asked. "What are you saying?"

Bragi tried to soothe her. "There is truth in Balder's dream. Some we know, and some we do not yet understand. Even a God cannot always know what is real and what is fantasy, or what is past and what is future."

Odin broke in. "Is there more to tell, Balder? Were

there other dreams?" Balder nodded but seemed reluctant to speak. "Tell us then," Odin persisted, "where did the third dream take place?"

"By the roots of the great ash Yggdrasil," Balder said. "It began by the tree of life, but when I first stood there I did not know where I was."

All of the Gods knew that Yggdrasil, the great world ash tree, had its branches touching heaven and its deepest root in hell, and that its trunk and limbs stretched through all the nine worlds. One of the three great roots of the tree was in Asgard over Urd's well. Urd, whose name meant Past, kept the tree green by sprinkling it with healing water from her spring; the dewy meadow where she sat was a sacred meeting place of the Gods. Yggdrasil's second root was in Jotunheim, the land of the giants, over the dark elf Mimir's well. In this murky pool wisdom and knowledge of good and evil and visions of the universe were stored.

The third root grew in Niflheim, the land of the dead. Underneath it was the spring called Hvergelmir, where serpents lived and from which many rivers flowed.

On Yggdrasil's highest branch sat an eagle who could watch the worlds of men and Gods. Four stags lived among the branches of the tree of life, eating its green leaves. A serpent called Nidhogg lived on the bank of the spring in Niflheim, gnawing at Yggdrasil's roots, sapping its strength. Up and down the tree Ratatosk the squirrel ran, carrying news and messages from the eagle in heaven to Nidhogg in hell, and back again.

"Near which root did the dream occur?" Odin asked Balder.

Balder hesitated, but Odin urged him to speak.

The Third Dream—I seemed to be a child, and I had gone for a walk in the hills in search of some treasure, but I knew not what. I walked in Midgard, the world of men, but everywhere I went people seemed not to know I was there. I asked questions, but no one listened or stopped what he was doing. I seemed to be in a hurry, but I did not know why. It was as if I were walking through a tapestry of history, being in it but not part of it. Nothing touched me. I saw and heard, but I was unseen.

I passed through a battlefield where so many men lay dying that all the grass was red. I said to a warrior on a well-armored horse, "Do you know where my treasure is hidden?" He did not answer, but drove his spear into the heart of a young boy who rode past me.

Suddenly it was midwinter, and snow and ice lay on all the farms and fields. I passed by two farmhouses close to each other, two farmyards with a fence between them. I saw two men who were brothers holding a sheep across the fence; one held its hind quarters, the other its forelegs, and they tugged and struggled and pulled the poor animal so hard it squealed in pain. I stopped beside the fence, and I said, "Do you know where my treasure is hidden?" but they did not hear my words. Then the snow was red with the blood of the sheep they had torn apart.

I looked to the sky, and on the hilltop was a beautiful stone castle where a king and his family lived. I knew then that I had not gone high enough in my searching, and so I hurried up the hill. The castle seemed to go farther and farther away from me as I climbed, and a storm cloud gathered thick and dark above. When I reached the place where the castle had been, the cloud was all about me.

31

Suddenly I heard someone laugh. It was not the laughter I hear in the courtyard on a sunny morning when the heroes meet in practice. It was not the laugh I heard when Idun and Bragi met after a long separation. It was not the sound of the young boy I heard galloping across a barley field on his pony, his hair flying in the breeze, his laugh high with the joy of speed and freedom. The sound was a pinched and eerie whine, squeezed from the tortured throat of some inhuman creature who knew more than he should and had seen more than he wanted. It was the laugh of a betrayer. It was the laugh of someone who knows he is soon to die—and is glad. Trembling, I looked around and found I was standing beneath an enormous tree at the edge of a pool of murky water. The hill I had climbed was the root itself, and the trunk of the tree was so wide and tall I could not see the top. I peered into the water, and at first all I saw were reflections of the black cloud. Then I saw a face in the water, and at first I thought it, too, was a reflection of my own, like seeing myself in death.

But the face was an old man's face, with transparent skin and wisps of gray hair that grew in patches and tufts from his gaunt cheeks and the two sides of his cleft chin. I thought, he is so old even his beard has grown bald! Suddenly I realized that the head floated on the water, quite by itself, bodyless.

"Do you know where my treasure is hidden?" I asked. The old head did not answer, but a hand appeared on the water nearby—just a hand, withered with skin drawn tight over bones, an armless appendage floating as the head did. Between the thumb and the forefinger something glittered, like a jewel. I wondered if at last I had found what I searched for.

But as the floating hand rotated the object, I knew it was no ordinary jewel chipped from the earth's black rock by a clever dwarf, but something far more rare; it was a glistening orb, translucent, and as the bony fingers turned it, they made just the slightest dent in its wet surface.

The old head laughed again, and with that soul-shaking sound I knew it was Mimir who laughed, Mimir the ancient dark elf who kept to himself the well of all knowledge of past and future, good and evil, hate and love. In his hand was Odin's other eye! I knew that some terrible bargain had been made between the Great Creator himself and this sinister dwarf, or else he would not laugh at me now.

Long ago, after the war with the Wanes—our closest neighbors and the friendly race from whom our gentle god Njord came to us—Odin must have known that though he was wise, he could not see far enough ahead nor back enough in time. I knew he had asked this old miser for a look into his well, and Mimir made Odin give up his eye. But did my father know how Mimir taunted me now with his treasure? I heard thunder from the treetop lost in the clouds.

The hand moved suddenly as if to throw that glistening orb at my head. "No!" I cried out in the gloom. "No, no, no!"

The vile waters cleared suddenly, and I saw the sun lying at the bottom of the pool. Then the storm broke around me with terrifying force, and a wind blew huge pellets of ice against my back. Bruised and sore, I tried to hide myself from the ice-stones that pelted me, and I covered my eyes from the blinding sight of the sun in Mimir's waters.

Nanna broke into Balder's story. "I woke him, for

34

he cried out loud, and he had curled himself into a ball of fear like a child hiding." Balder sat silent, exhausted, as if the telling had been as terrible as the dreaming.

The Gods were silent for a moment, and then they all began to talk at once.

Frigga said, "Odin, what did you learn from the elf when you looked into his well? What terrible secrets do you keep from us all?"

Thor buckled his girdle of strength and pulled on his gloves. "Tell us, Father-of-All, you who have spent your life searching for wisdom and knowledge of the world and its ways, what do these dreams mean? Whose life is threatened? Where are the enemies that we must fight? I'm not afraid of any giant, or any dark elf for that matter. With my hammer, Mjollnir, I can whip the strongest giant or smash the highest mountain."

One-handed Tyr, the god of war to whom no man looked for peace or reconciliation, said, "If it had been me at the well, I would have killed him for threatening me like that. You can't let demons survive! Stamp them out! Cut off their heads—"

Bragi broke in gently, and all listened as they so often did to his voice and the words that came like melodies from his lips. "This dream says more than meets the mind. Odin, search your memory; ask your ravens. Where have you in past or other worlds heard tell of the doings in Balder's dreams? We well know his own mind did not create these images, for it is the nature of Balder that no sinful or impure thought can enter his heart."

Hoder, who had been silent for a long time, said, "If my brother's life is threatened, let it be mine that is taken. I would follow him anywhere and every-

35

where he goes, for it is in his laughter that I find joy, and through his eyes I see the world."

"Hush," Frigga said. "Your mind leaps much too fast, Hoder. Why should Balder's life be threatened? He has done no harm. Perhaps there is some other danger his dreams foretell."

The timid god, Hoenir, said, "There are many places where a blind brother cannot follow, Hoder. Yet how unfair it must seem to you! Inequality does lead to jealousy, and jealousy to greed, and among men at least, greed leads to war. All those were in Balder's dream, yet we know none can be in his own mind."

"I know that," Hoder said, then turned to Odin. "What did you see in Mimir's well, Great Father? Can you go again to the bodyless one and look?"

All the Gods then waited for Odin to speak. Finally he said, "I can go to Mimir's well, and even farther. Now let us meet in the council hall, away from this feasting place, and give me your wisest thoughts."

The high Gods followed Odin to Gladsheim, and there they talked all the night. Nanna and Balder went to their home, Breidablik, which nothing unclean could enter.

It was nearly dawn when the Gods decided that Odin should go down to Niflheim and speak once more with the wise woman who was buried there and learn what Balder's nightmares would mean for them.

5: THE DEAD WISE WOMAN SPEAKS

Then Odin rode to the eastern door.
There he knew well was the wise woman's grave;
Magic he spoke, and mighty charms,
Till spellbound she rose,
And in death she spoke.

Before the sun herself appeared over the eastern ocean, Odin saddled his gray stallion, Sleipnir, which was the finest and fastest of all the horses in Asgard. Sleipnir had eight legs and could fly over land or sea. He could go as swiftly as the wind and as high as the stars. When his eight hooves galloped over Bifrost, the rainbow bridge between Asgard and Midgard, the sound could be heard from heaven to hell.

Sleipnir had been given to Odin by Loki, who had mothered the wonderful horse in a strange adventure. It happened after the war with the Wanes when the walls of Asgard were broken down. Odin was always loath to think about that first war, because the Wanes were friends of the Gods, their closest neighbors, and Odin's part in the war had not been wise or compassionate. After peace had been made, all agreed, however, that the Gods must protect them-

37

selves from invaders, and the wall had to be rebuil
A giant disguised as a stonemason came to Od
and offered to build a new wall, creating a fortress
Asgard, in just one year. For payment he asked thr
gifts: the goddess Freyja, the sun, and the moon.

Odin called the Gods to council. They needed t
fortress, but Asgard was so large they did not believ
one man could finish a surrounding wall in one yea
Loki persuaded the Gods to accept the offer, and t
contract was made on condition that the maso
have the help of no man.

"I need no helper," the laborer told Odin, "b
allow me my horse, Svadilfari. He is all I want."

The Gods agreed and then watched the work pr
gress. During the day, the man worked slowly, car
fully fitting stone on stone with tireless skill. B
during the night, the wall seemed to grow alarming
fast. What the Gods did not know at first was th
the horse, Svadilfari, was wonderfully talented, ar
could move stones as large as hills in a single nigh
Summer approached. The fortress was nearly done

Frigga said to Odin, "What will you do if he finish
before summer? I suppose we could survive withou
Freyja, but without the sun we will all die! The wal
grow while the Gods are asleep!"

Odin frowned, and remembering that he had a
cepted the bargain on Loki's advice, called the clev
one to Gladsheim. "What is the secret of the nigh
working horse?" he asked.

Loki said without hesitating, "He is a giant
magic horse, and will finish the wall within t
month."

"How could you let us agree to such a contract
you knew this mason was a giant?" Odin asked.

Loki shrugged. "You wanted the wall. He coul

38

build it. I did not think it mattered what we promised."

Odin drew himself up and said angrily, "We Gods cannot break our word! Do not make that mistake again. Get rid of this horse, for we must not lose Freyja, the sun, or the moon!"

That night Loki disguised himself as a mare and came near Svadilfari. As the stallion dragged an enormous boulder up the hill toward the place in the wall where the mason worked, Loki whinnied softly.

The stallion sniffed the air and pawed the ground. Loki whinnied again. Svadilfari stopped.

"Get back to work!" the giant roared at his horse.

But Loki whinnied once more softly, saying, "Come with me," and trotted toward the woods.

Svadilfari dropped the rope; the boulder rolled back down the hill, and the stallion galloped deep into the woods after the mare. For days and days the two horses played together, and the giant could not find them.

Summer came. The sun reached its highest point, and the nights were so short and so light that even at midnight the Gods could see the mason hard at work, piling stone on stone. But without Svadilfari's help he could not finish the wall on time, and the Gods did not have to give up their goddess of golden tears or their source of light.

In the autumn, after the leaves had blown off the trees, the mare foaled, and Loki returned to Asgard with a wonderful gray eight-legged horse trotting behind him. He gave this best horse of all to Odin, and it was called Sleipnir.

Now as Odin began his long journey to Niflheim, he passed over Midgard, the land of men. He looked

39

down on a familiar scene and was pleased. Nestled in an isolated but still verdant valley below was a group of sheep farms. The men and women who owned them kept to themselves and raised their children well. Every spring the young boys would drive the sheep from all the farms into the high, long meadows that stretched like great green carpets between the craggy ridges of the mountain. There the sheep would wander free to graze on the grass that grew so thick and strong during the long summer days and bright summer nights. Now and then during the summer a young shepherd would check the flocks and see that the lambs were healthy and with their mothers.

Odin noticed a young boy on a high rock staring at him as he flew across the valley. The Greatest God waved to the boy, and after a moment the child waved back. Then he raced down the mountainside, slipping and sliding on the loose stones, laughing and shouting, "I saw him! I saw him! Ten legs . . . three eyes . . . one tail . . . I saw him!" Odin smiled at the sight and then turned his eye once more toward the northern ice, past the furnaces the giant Surt tended over the worlds where once the steaming gap had been.

As Sleipnir carried Odin toward Niflheim, land of the dead, Odin thought of the visions of evil he had seen in Mimir's well, and he knew the trade had been worth the cost. Though his sight with one eye lacked dimension, he knew his enemies. That was half the battle, he thought, to know whom you must fight.

Hadn't it always been so! From the beginning of time that had been the core of every challenge that had confronted him. Sometimes those who had seemed most dangerous at first turned out to be harmlessly loud. Sometimes those whom he had trusted were betrayers; and those whom he distrusted bestowed the greatest gifts. Even Sleipnir, he thought fondly, stroking the gray steed's mane, had been a gift of the god who was most mischievous and disloyal.

More swiftly than Odin's own thoughts the nine worlds went by, and suddenly in front of him there was such a howling and barking that Sleipnir reared and neighed in terror. Standing in the path was a thick-bodied hound, with huge feet planted squarely and broad head thrown back. His chest was bloody and his teeth bared.

"Ride on," Odin said to his frightened horse. "That is only Garm, the hound of Hel. The noisy beast cannot harm us."

Sleipnir galloped so fast that the high gates of hell were still shaking when Odin came to them. There at the eastern entrance he was startled to see that the normally gloomy place was strung with garlands of dead flowers and leaves and decorated with golden ornaments as if preparations for a popular feast were going on. Odin did not go inside the gates, for no live man or God entered there. But he climbed down from Sleipnir's back and searched in the mists for the grave he had visited once before. He held the hood of his cloak over his forehead to hide his single eye, and called loudly for the Vala to rise from her grave. He said magic words that would draw her from death.

The first time he called, the mist on the grave stirred, but the wise woman did not appear.

He called her again. Garm howled in the distance, but the Vala did not appear.

Odin called a third time. Then the mists swirled

about him and a damp wind that smelled of mountain moss and mold blew across his face. A figure appeared in the vapors before him, a pale collection of bones and withered skin, with blank hollows where eyes once had been. Swaying as if spellbound, she spoke to him, and her voice was like the merest crackling of dry leaves.

She said:

> "What is the man to me unknown
> That has made me travel the troublous road?
> I was snowed on with snow, and smitten with rain,
> And drenched with dew; long was I dead."

Odin kept his eye hidden, for he knew the dead woman was of the giant race and would not tell the truth to any god. He gave a strange name, and he spoke in measured phrases.

> "Vegtam my name, I am Valtam's son.
> Speak to me of hell, for of heaven I know.
> For whom are the benches bright with rings
> And the platforms gay, bedecked with gold?"

The Vala said:

> "Here for Balder the mead is brewed.
> Unwilling I spoke, and now would be still."

So Balder's nightmare had meant his death, and the fires he had seen had been his own balefire, his funeral flames! That was what Odin had feared. Still not revealing his true identity, he said:

> "Wise woman, cease not. Tell me all I need to know.
> Who shall the bane of Balder become
> And steal the life of Odin's son?"

The Vala said:

> "Hoder bears the far-famed branch;
> He shall the bane of Balder become

43

And steal the life of Odin's son.
Unwilling I spoke, and now would be still."

Quickly Odin said:

"Wise woman, cease not! There is more I need
    to know.
Who shall avenge this evil work?"

The figure swayed and retreated, and for a moment Odin was afraid she would speak no more. But finally she said:

"Rind bears Vali in Vestrsalir and
One night old fights Odin's son.
His hands he shall wash not, his hair shall comb not,
Till the slayer of Balder he brings to the flame."

Odin stood in stunned silence. The wind blew about him, and his hood fell away from his forehead. Suddenly the cracked voice spoke angrily:

"You are not Vegtam as I thought before.
Odin you are, the enchanter old!"

Odin answered with equal fury:

"You are no wise woman, nor have you wisdom.
Mother of three giants is all you are. Liar!
I will not believe all you say."

The Vala rose and swayed and then seemed to shrink before his eyes.

"Ride home, Odin, be ever proud.
No man or god shall hear my voice again
Until Ragnarok, the last and final battle!"

Then there was only the damp wind, the vapor, and in Odin's mind the sound of the Vala's words went round and round.

6: THE FENRIS WOLF

By the mouth of the river the wolf remains
Till the Gods to destruction go.

Riding back across the spans of black, bleak mountains and ice-filled valleys, Odin thought of what he had heard. He had gone to the Vala to learn the truth, and she had said such terrible things to him that he wanted not to believe them. And as he flew toward Valhalla, he thought of the many generations of men and Gods gone by since he had begun the world. He watched the sun set over the dying landscape, painting a feeble pink fringe on the sharp, icy peaks. In the pale light it seemed the long winter had already come. Odin wondered how many times that spark from the fire world he had set on its way would rise again if the Vala spoke the truth. With Balder's death, Odin knew, the Fimbul, or everlasting, winter would be upon them. Already the days were short, and it seemed as if the sun were so tired she could hardly go her brief way across the southern sky before she fell below the earth again.

For a long time Odin had known about and feared Ragnarok, the final destruction, but he had always strived against it. As long as he was able to keep the evil forces leashed, man and God could survive, though they had suffered. But Hel was ready for Balder's arrival! That he had not known. Did Frigga know what Balder's dreams meant? Did she know that if Balder died all the monsters in the universe would be loosed? There was much in the ways of the world that his wife knew and did not tell, but would she believe the Vala's words? Odin did not know the answers to those questions, nor to many others he asked himself. Could he stop the final battle from coming? And if so, how?

Odin thought of his many names—among them Great-Creator, All-Father, Father-of-the-Slain, Knower-of-Many-Things, Fulfiller-of-Wishes, Protector-of-Men, Maker-of-the-Greatest-Magic, Seer-of-All-Truths—but he knew that with all of his wisdom and insight and power he might not be able to save the life of his most pure and beautiful son, and of the world.

From the beginning, since Bergelmir had escaped over the oceans of Ymir's blood, Odin had crushed the evil giant's descendants, who threatened his family of men and Gods. But now the Vala had said to him that Hoder, his own son, would be the god-destroyer! It could not be!

So often, it seemed to him, his messengers, his sons, his warriors, did not fulfill his wishes. He had made the world, and he had made men in it, and he had made the Gods, and he had made warriors to fight the giants, but he could not always control what he had made.

In the morning of time, the first threat to the Gods had been the birth of Loki's son, Fenrir, also called the Fenris Wolf. The Gods took the wolf pup into Asgard to raise, but soon he was so big that only the bravest god, Tyr, dared to come close enough to feed and care for him. Fenrir trusted Tyr and would not hurt him. The wolf pup ate and grew and ate and grew. The larger it grew, the more frightened the Gods became. Finally they realized that when Fenrir opened his mouth, his lower jaw was on the earth and his upper jaw touched the sky.

"You must chain the wolf," Frigga said to Odin. "He could swallow us all!"

Loki said, "Let him be. He has harmed no one."

Hoenir, the timid god who often joined Odin on his travels around the world, said, "But what if he becomes angry? He could swallow heaven and earth! We can't let such a monster go free."

The Goddesses agreed when they saw how much Fenrir ate each day and how wide his jaws were. One tooth alone was as tall as a spruce tree.

"What do you think?" Odin asked Balder.

"The only beasts that frighten me are frightened beasts," Balder replied. "I have never know an animal that did not respond to love."

Frigga smiled at Balder's kind words. But Sif, Thor's wife, was not so calm. She said, "But Balder, even you would die if the wolf snapped his jaws. Who knows what might enrage him?"

Balder did not hear what Sif said, for he had wandered down to the rainbow bridge where he liked to chat with Heimdall, the watchman of the Gods and guardian of the bridge. Frigga watched Balder go, knowing that no impure or angry thought could enter her first son's head.

Odin listened to the anxious voices around him. Finally he ordered the Gods to make a chain strong enough to bind the wolf pup. Fenrir was docile enough when they put the chain on him. But as soon as it was secure, he stretched his legs and the chain broke apart. The Gods then forged another chain, twice as thick as the first, and out of a metal twice as strong. Again Fenrir let them put it on him, knowing that if he broke the heavy irons he would be famous. When the last link was tight, he dashed himself against a rock-faced mountain and the chain burst. Fragments flew far and wide. The Gods were alarmed, for not only was the wolf the most powerful creature that had ever lived in Asgard, but he knew his own strength. Everyone but Tyr and Loki and Balder lived in terror of Fenrir's shadow, his temper, and his strength so long as he was free.

Odin called the high council together. He said they must make a new kind of chain, of more powerful substance than any thought of before. "This wolf," he said, "though tender enough in spirit because of his youth, has the power to destroy us all. Therefore, we must devise a fetter that is not ordinary. If magic has made him grow so large, then only magic will confine him. Balder, I charge you with the task of finding such a chain."

Balder said, "I have carved beautiful handles for my tools, and I have polished stones until they gleamed. I have walked among men and children and made them laugh at the sight of two birds courting. I sat with a six-year-old boy and counted his flock of sheep. But never have I fought any man or beast, nor do I know of such things. Why do you think I can make a chain?"

48

Odin said, "The strength of your happiness will match any other in earth or heaven."

Bragi spoke up. "Odin is right. The Fenris Wolf cannot be bound by ordinary means. There are some dwarfs I know who may help us. We are all in danger of this monstrous puppy! Come, Balder, we will find something with which to bind the wolf."

When Balder and Bragi returned to Asgard, the Gods and Goddesses crowded around to see what they had brought, but their hands were empty.

"Bring Fenrir to the field," Bragi said to Tyr, "and let us try our new chain on him."

"But you have nothing in your hands," Tyr said surprised.

"This chain is called Gleipnir," Balder said. "And you cannot see it or feel it except in anger. Trust Bragi. He knows what he is doing."

Tyr brought the Fenris Wolf to the big field between Valhalla and Gladsheim, and the Gods and Goddesses met him there. When Fenrir saw them all waiting he became suspicious and growled and would have turned away. Tyr urged him forward.

"Stay still, Fenrir," the brave god coaxed. "Let Bragi try this new chain on you. They think it is the strongest ever made, but you have broken all the others, so you need not be afraid. You know how strong you are. You know that Bragi is wise and gentle, and Balder is good and gentle, and neither would hurt you!"

The wolf eyed the two gods and nervously licked his jaws. "Will you take the chain off me if I cannot break it?" he asked.

"Yes," Tyr said without hesitation. "But if you cannot see it, why be afraid?"

"How do I know you will remove it?" Fenrir asked the one who fed him.

"I will put my hand in your mouth," Tyr said. "If I did not mean to keep my word, I would not dare! You will lie still and let us put the chain called Gleipnir around you. It will be another test of your strength."

The wolf lay still, and Tyr put his hand in the huge young jaws. Bragi tied Gleipnir, the invisible chain, around and about Fenrir's legs and over his back, and made a harness across his chest. Then with Thor's help he pulled it tight.

Fenrir felt bound, and he strained against the fetters he could not see. Warily he looked around at the tense faces of the Gods. Thor pulled harder. Fenrir growled and twisted and tried to break the bonds. But he could not do it.

"Let me loose," he growled. "I cannot break this chain. What is it made of? Why is it so strong? My father told me never to trust a God, and I do not trust you now." He thrashed against his invisible bonds.

The Gods smiled in relief. The more Fenrir struggled, the tighter he seemed to be bound. Gleipnir was strong enough.

"Let me go!" Fenrir howled in outraged anger, his cries reaching to the ends of heaven. "Tyr, do not betray me!"

The Gods would not let Fenrir loose, for now he was truly angry and more fearsome than ever. When the wolf pup knew that he could not be free, he clamped his jaws tight and bit off Tyr's right hand.

The Gods took the bound wolf to an island in the middle of a large lake and tied Gleipnir to a huge boulder. They left the Fenris Wolf there forever, writhing, twisting, crying in fury and pain, but unable to harm anyone.

"That is a marvelously strong chain," Frigga said to Bragi when they returned. "What is it made of?"

"Six things," Bragi replied. "The sound of a cat's step, the beards of women, the roots of mountains, the nerves of bears, the breath of fishes, and the spittle of birds."

"But those are nothing," Thor said. "Nonsense! What magic is that?"

Hoder laughed. "Thor can only believe what he sees. But Fenrir, like me, now knows the strength of what he believes. And for once I am not the only one who is blind," he added quietly.

Hoder's voice had been lighthearted—or had it? Was it possible that the Vala was right? Could Hoder be jealous of Balder as well as loving? How like his dark-browed son to perceive the invisible truths when others could only believe what they could touch and see, Odin thought, spurring Sleipnir on high above the dark evergreen forests of Jotunheim.

*No truce made Balder's
   brother
With the bitter foe of eartl
   folk.*

*Rocks shook, and crags
   shivered.
I saw the giant waver and
   give way...
Fast before the giant-slaye*

Riding on Sleipnir's back out of the lands of darkness, Odin crossed the nine worlds as if they were layers in time. Though the trip back to Valhalla was no more arduous and took no longer than the way to Niflheim, though Sleipnir was swift and strong, some of the memories that flooded Odin's mind were long and some were painful. He saw the tired old sun still trying to make its way across the world, and he thought:

Oh, spark that once I set into the sky, keeper of light and growing life for men and Gods, without you we will all die! The Vala saw you fallen; the giant's wolf wants to swallow you; the ancient dark elf waits to receive you! Why haven't my worthy defenders of the world defeated your antagonists?

Odin thought of the battles he and his faithful warriors had fought and won against the giants so that men could raise their children, grow their crops, and enjoy the beauties of the world in peace and freedom and without fear. But giants still harassed the Gods, and though many had been killed, peace had not been won. If only he could have proved once and for all, Odin thought, that the Gods were superior, Thor might never have had to fight another giant!

There was no doubt in Odin's mind that Thor was the best giant-killer. With his magic belt he had divine strength and could wade through the deepest rivers. With his gloves on he could wield his mountain-splitting hammer, which some dwarfs had made for the Gods long ago. When lightning flashed over Midgard and thunder roared and rocks split open, men said it was Thor in his godly wrath throwing his hammer, Mjollnir, at some giant enemy. Odin could not count the number of giants who had fallen before Thor's hammer. And so long ago, it had been Thor whom Odin chose to challenge the king of all giants to a contest to prove the superiority of the Gods.

"Go to the east," Odin had instructed Thor. "Find Utgard-Loki, the king of the giants, and tell him I sent you. Beware, however, for Utgard-Loki is a master at magic, hard to find and still harder to deal with. You must be clever, as well as strong, and you may need help."

Thor asked Loki to go with him, for Loki, though often untrustworthy, was clever at magic and knew the ways of the giant world well. Thor also took along his two servant children, Thjalfi and his sister Roskva.

The four challengers from Asgard, Odin remembered, travelled far beyond the sea that separated Asgard from Jotunheim. The first day they walked through an endless forest. When night came, they were too tired to eat so they looked for a safe place to sleep. In a clearing near the edge of the pine woods, they came to a strangely shaped structure, not quite like a dome and not quite like a castle—a mound of a house that had an entrance as wide as four horses but not so tall. The Gods cautiously crept inside and found themselves in a cavernous room with curved walls all lined with some animal's soft skin. They lay down together against one of the walls and soon fell asleep.

In the middle of the night they were wakened by a whistling and crashing and rumbling, and the walls shook so violently that they thought there must be an earthquake. Odin's brave warriors clung together until the quake was over. Then, hoping to find some safer place to sleep, Thor led his little band through the darkness, feeling his way along the soft wall until he came to a small side chamber, a narrow curved hall that stopped abruptly and led to no other rooms. Thjalfi and Roskva and Loki slept inside this dark place, and Thor stretched himself across the entrance so that he could protect them all.

In the morning, when he could sleep no more, Thor found his way out of the strange house. There under the trees, filling the space of an eighty-man seagoing ship, was a giant stretched out on the ground, fast asleep. His brass belt-buckle was as big as a bull's head, and it rose and fell as the giant breathed. He was snoring so loudly that Thor realized to his shame what the "earthquake" had been. He buckled his girdle of strength and summoned his courage. He climbed a tree near the giant's head and raised his hammer over the enormous forehead.

The giant opened his bright green eyes.

Thor's courage failed him for the first time, and he lowered his hammer. Cautiously he said, "What is your name?"

"Skrymir," the giant replied, sitting up so his head reached over the treetops. "But I know who you are," he said, looking down at Thor, who clung to the pine branch. "You are the formidable god Thor. I have heard many mighty stories about you."

Thor was flattered and pleased.

"But what have you done with my mitten?" Skrymir reached out his hand and, to Thor's chagrin, picked up an enormous mitten that was lying nearby. Thor realized that the safe, small room they had found to sleep in during the night was the mitten's thumb!

Jovially Skrymir said, "Have you eaten? Let us share our provisions." Thor, not wanting to make such a large giant angry, climbed down from the tree and called his servant boy Thjalfi to open his bag of food. Hiding behind Thor, Thjalfi did as he was told. Skrymir then scooped up all of the Gods' food, put it in his own bag, threw it over his shoulder, and in three strides was out of the forest and beyond the next hill.

Thor was disgusted. Everyone was hungry. The woods were all pine, and nothing edible grew in their shade, so the Gods followed Skrymir's tracks. It was night before the two children, Loki, and Thor, panting with hunger and thirst, found Skrymir sitting placidly beside an oak tree.

"I thought you would never get here," the giant said grinning at them. "Whatever took you so long? You must be starved."

Thor did not answer. "Here." Skrymir handed him

the bag. "Take the food for I have already eaten. I'll go on to sleep if you don't mind."

The giant stretched out and soon was snoring so loudly that again it seemed as if the earth would break apart. But Thor had no fear of the sound now. He picked up the giant's bag and tried to untie the leather thong that bound it. The thong was strangely stiff, and Thor could not undo the knot.

"Here," he said to Loki, "see if you can untie this. We have to eat, or we will never be able to travel tomorrow."

Loki tugged at the leather strings, but his slender fingers could not bend one of them even a little, much less untie them. "There is something strange about the knot," he told Thor, "but I don't know what it is." Then Roskva, the little servant girl, tried, but the thongs were hard and hurt her fingers so she cried.

"Never mind," said Thor angrily. "I know it's useless. We've been tricked, and I was stupid and helpless. Go to sleep, and I'll take care of the monster my own way for sure this time."

"Be careful," Loki cautioned. "I don't understand his magic yet."

"Don't worry," Thor said, and climbed the oak tree. When he was high enough and surely out of sight, he raised his hammer. This time he aimed carefully and swung Mjollnir as hard as he could onto the giant's forehead. The oak tree trembled when the blow struck, and Thor nearly fell off the branch.

Skrymir opened one eye lazily and said in a puzzled voice, "I do think a leaf must have fallen on my head." He opened the other eye and looked around. "Where are you, Thor?" The giant looked up and suddenly Thor saw those green eyes staring straight at him. Skrymir grinned. "Have you eaten yet? Aren't you ever going to sleep?"

Feeling foolish, Thor climbed down out of the tree and told Skrymir that he had been too tired to eat. "I was just getting my bearings before settling down for the night." Skrymir raised one eyebrow at Thor's explanation. Thor did not want to test the giant's temper now, nor did he want to admit that he had been tricked out of his dinner. "We need rest more than food, " Thor continued. "We'll eat with you in the morning."

Then Thor stretched himself out near Skrymir's mountainous shoulder and closed his eyes, but he did not sleep. He waited until midnight, when Skrymir's snores again reached a thunderous peak. Then Thor swung Mjollnir so high and brought it down so fast and felt it sink so deep, that he knew no creature could survive such a blow.

Skrymir sat up and rubbed his eyes. "Oh," he said sleepily, "something woke me up. I think an acorn must have hit me." He turned to Thor cheerfully and said, "Have you slept well?"

Thor was speechless. Never had he felt so foolish, never so angry, so powerless! He clenched his fist around the handle of the hammer that had failed him. How could Skrymir be alive? What had happened to Mjollnir's power and to his own strength? Only recently he had smashed a stone-headed giant at least as big as Skrymir. How could this arrogant creature be alive still?

"What is the matter?" Skrymir persisted. "Didn't you hear me? I asked if you had slept well."

"Oh, no, I mean yes," Thor stammered, trying to recover his dignity. He certainly did not want Skrymir to know his own misgivings. "I slept well until you woke me just now."

"What time is it?" the giant asked. "It must be nearly dawn."

"Just midnight," Thor said. "There is still half a night to sleep."

Skrymir closed his eyes once more, but it was a long time before Thor heard his breathing become even. If he could just catch Skrymir in one more deep moment of sleep, Thor thought, perhaps he could finish the villain off. Just before dawn the regular rumbling snores began again. Thor took up another notch in his belt, took a firmer hold of Mjollnir. Three times 'round his head he swung the trusted hammer before he let it fly to the cheek of the sleeping giant.

Skrymir sat up, and Thor nearly fell off the tree in surprise. But the giant simply rubbed his cheek where the hammer had hit, and Thor thought he saw a faint smile around Skrymir's mouth.

"Mmm," said the giant, frowning, "I do believe a bird must have stopped to rest in a branch over my face." He looked at Thor, who felt very small suddenly, and not very strong. "Well, I have had better nights than that. Did you sleep well?" he asked Thor again.

Thor nodded. Skrymir stood up, stretched, picked up the bag with all the Gods' food still in it, and put it over his shoulder. Thor and Loki and the children wanted desperately to beg him to open the bag, to give them something to eat before he left, but none of them dared speak. Hungrily they looked at the sack so high above their heads.

Skrymir smiled down at the unhappy group and said, "Well, better get started if you want to meet our giant-king today. There's a long walk ahead of you." He gazed over the rolling hills, then looked down at Thor again. "Let me give you a bit of advice, Thor. I wouldn't go into Utgard-Loki's castle boasting, if I were you. He does not favor braggarts, and he is a lot larger, stronger, and more ill-tempered than I am." Skrymir turned away, but over his shoulder he tossed one last message. "My best advice is to go back to the west and forget about Utgard-Loki." In three easy steps the green-eyed giant was so far away he looked like a tiny stick on the top of the farthest hill.

Hungry, sleepy, but still determined to do their best to find the king of the giants as Odin had ordered them to, Thor and his travelers turned again toward the east and began the long walk over the sunburned hills.

8: THE KING
OF THE GIANTS

A man shall not boast of his
*   keenness of mind*
But keep it close to his chest.
To the silent and wise does ill
*   seldom come*
When he goes to a house as
*   a guest.*

At noon the hot, tired Gods stopped to rest near a boulder in the middle of a sun-baked plain. Suddenly across the sand a cloud of dust rose, and when it cleared, a great stone castle stood before them. It loomed so high they lay on their backs to see the top.

"Let's go," Thor said, and led his group through the iron grating that surrounded the castle, down a long straight path to a pair of huge iron doors that stood open. The Gods found themselves inside a vaulted hall, lit only by shafts of light that came down from openings high in the arched roof. They stood and blinked, and when their eyes grew accustomed to the dimness, they saw the hall was lined with benches. Even Thor caught his breath when he realized that the men and women on the benches were all nearly as big as Skrymir.

Thor led Loki and the children down the center aisle, and the giants stared silently at the travelers all the way to the end of the hall. Thor thought, as he approached the giant-king's throne, that Valhalla, the dining hall, and his own home—Bilskirnir—with its five hundred and forty rooms, were the largest buildings he had known. But this throne room of Utgard-Loki was longer and higher than all of his rooms together.

Suddenly Thor stopped. In front of his nose was a large, furry knee. He looked up. He saw two great elbows on the arms of an elaborately carved chair. He looked up higher and saw the face of the king, Utgard-Loki himself, a magnificent bearded figure with long yellow hair and furry hands as big as a bear's body. Thor stepped back so he could look up to the giant's face, and he saluted the king in a dignified manner.

Utgard-Loki's voice was rough like the growl of a bear. "Who is this toddler who stands by my left shoe? Is it the great god Thor? How tiny he is! I cannot believe he is as strong as he says."

Thor tugged at his gloves and tightened his belt. "I am the first son of Odin, the Great Creator," he said proudly, "and my father's strongest god. My mother was Jord, the earth herself." Thor spoke in his deepest voice. He was sure of his might, but he knew that in order to defeat *this* giant he would need sharp wits as well.

Utgard-Loki grunted and said, "You have forced your way into my castle." The giant's tone was not playful now, but ominous. "I let no one stay here alive who is not talented either in strength or magic. Tell me, Thor, what can the son of Odin and Jord do? What feats can you or your small friends perform? You have boasted of your great strength—let us see you show it!"

Thor took a deep breath. He spoke in firm, round tones, neither boastfully nor fearfully, for he wanted to be worthy of Odin. "It is the All-Father's wish that we show you remarkable feats of strength and endurance that will prove even to one so large and intelligent as you that the Gods, though small in stature, are great in strength and power; and that if in this contest you agree to the superiority of the Gods, you will leave us and all men of Odin's creation in peace forever."

Utgard-Loki tapped on the arm of his chair with his furry finger, and the sound in Thor's ear was as loud as a bass drum. Finally the king said, "What will you do?"

Loki spoke up bravely. "I suggest that there is no one here who can eat as much or as quickly as I."

Utgard-Loki snapped his fingers. Immediately a servant brought in a long wooden trough filled with freshly roasted meat. The king then said, "Let the giant Logi come forward!" As Logi walked the length of the hall, the giants on the benches gave him wide berth. Though he was not so large as some, his face was very red, and he seemed to give off a great amount of heat. Utgard put him at one end of the trough, and the clever god Loki at the other. "Eat," he commanded the two of them, and the contest began.

Logi and Loki gobbled the fresh meat. Loki, so hungry from the long journey, ate wonderfully fast, and when he met Logi in the middle there was not a scrap or morsel of food behind him, nor meat on any of the bones. But the giant had devoured meat, bones,

63

and even the trough itself! It did seem to all, even to Thor, that Loki had lost the contest.

Utgard-Loki raised one bushy eyebrow and smiled out of one side of his wide mouth. "Well," he said to Thor, "Perhaps you will do better in the next contest. What can your little man do?" He pointed his furry finger at Thjalfi. The little boy trembled, but Thor beckoned him forward.

"He is the fastest runner in the world," Thor said proudly.

The king said, "Let him race with my servant Hugi." Thjalfi came to the king's throne, and the race began. They raced from the throne to the door of the hall and back again. In the first heat Hugi reached the throne before Thjalfi was halfway back from the door. "Thjalfi will have to do better than that to beat my runner," the king growled. "let them try another course."

Thor patted Thjalfi on the shoulder and told him not to be afraid. This time he would do better.

In the second heat, Hugi turned back from the door before Thjalfi was halfway there. Thor frowned but said, "Let him try again." In the third and last race, Thjalfi was so tired that he had hardly started down the aisle before Hugi was back at Utgard-Loki's throne. Thor's child-servant fell down exhausted on the bench between the defeated Loki and an enormous giant whose face was as cold and hard and chiseled as an iceberg.

Utgard-Loki did not discuss the race, but Thor, ashamed of the poor performance of his servants, said, "The next feats will be my own. First I will drink in contest with anyone of your choosing. Bring me a horn."

The king raised his eyebrow again and snapped

his fingers. "Bring the soldier's horn," he bellowed, and to Thor he said, "It is the largest in Jotunheim. Here we are accustomed to saying that a good man can drain this horn in one breath, but some do need two. No one here is so poor a drinker that he fails to drain it in three."

The horn was carried in by two giants. It was so large that Thor had to let it rest on the ground, for he could not hold it in the air. But he was not worried, for his thirst was great. He put the horn to his lips and began to drink.

The giant with the icy face said to Thjalfi, "Is Thor really so strong as everyone says? Never have I heard a less modest fighter speak!"

Thjalfi said, yes, his master was every bit as strong as his reputation.

"And what of his famous hammer?" the giant inquired. "Does his great might vanish when his hammer is gone?"

"Oh, no," Thjalfi said loyally, "but I have never seen Thor without it," he added, watching his master take the liquid from the horn.

Thor could hold his breath long, and for this feat he had taken a deep one, drinking all he could of the lusty liquid, filling his mouth and throat with more and more. It seemed as he drank that the horn should have emptied faster. But finally his breath ran out and he had to swallow. The horn seemed nearly as full as it had been when he began.

Thjalfi's heart began to beat harder as he watched Thor. Utgard-Loki said, "Try again," and smiled confidently at the giants on the benches. "Thor did all right, but there is still a lot left."

Discouraged but valiant, Thor took another deep, long, exhausting swallow from the horn. Again, when his breath ran out, it seemed there was nearly as much liquid left as when he started. Unhappily he remembered the king's warning, that there was no one in Jotunheim who failed to drain it in three swallows! Thor tried to drain the horn in the third draught; it was the longest held breath, the greatest amount that he had ever taken, and he drank until he thought his lungs and throat would burst. Then he stopped. There was some difference in the amount of liquid in the horn. He could see clearly that the level was lower, but there was still much left.

Thor handed the horn back to Utgard-Loki and announced, "I will drink no more."

The king nodded. "Well, you are not quite so great a drinker as you thought. Perhaps not greater than the giants after all. But maybe you can do something else to show off your strength. Come, lift my cat so that all four feet are off the ground."

Thor watched a gray cat with tail high and back arched walk onto the floor near him. The cat purred and rubbed against the king's foot. It was a very large cat by men's standards, as large as a wolf perhaps, but next to these creatures certainly not formidable. Thor had grappled easily with much larger beasts, bears and horses and boars. He put his hand under the soft gray belly and tried to lift the cat. The animal arched its back at Thor's touch. Thor put both hands under the cat and lifted it higher. The cat's back curved higher. The higher Thor pulled, the greater the arch; and though there was no weight to lift, there seemed to be no way he could get the cat's four paws off the floor. Once again Thor, whose pride was so great, had to admit defeat.

Utgard-Loki said casually, "I thought perhaps you were apt to overstate your talents. Accept the fact now that the Gods are small and weak compared to my people!"

Thor was angry. He was sure the giant was using magic against him. If only he could match strength for strength! He said, "Little as you call me, I will show you not magic, but pure might. I will wrestle with any one of you—no matter how large. I will prove my strength!"

The king smiled and nodded again. "All right, but I will not make it too difficult. See if you can win a fair match with this old woman, Elli. She used to be my nursemaid, but always could throw a man bigger than you to the floor."

A withered old woman came in, tall enough, but so lacking in muscle or youth that Thor was ashamed to touch her. "I cannot fight a woman," he said indignantly, "much less an old and feeble one like her."

"She is stronger than you think," the king said. "Go ahead and try to force her to the floor."

Reluctantly Thor put his hands on the two frail arms. To his surprise he found them like steel rods. He pushed the woman a little, and she did not bend. Then he began to summon his strength, but the harder he struggled to down her, the more firmly rooted she stood. He could not bend nor sway the old hag though now he fought her desperately. Where was the mighty power Odin had given him in the morning of time when he was born? Tears came to Thor's eyes, and his breath was short, and suddenly he swayed and fell to one knee. The contest was over. Thor walked in deepest shame back to the bench where Loki and the children waited for him. "Let's go," he said angrily. But he did not know how he would face the All-Father and his brothers in Asgard again.

"Stay the night," Utgard-Loki called to them. "You must rest before your journey home." One of the giant servants showed the gods to a comfortable room in the castle and left them with cheerful wishes for a good night's sleep.

In the morning they were about to leave when they found a huge feasting table laid out with plenty of food and drink. The king's servant told them to eat, and they fell to with relish. When they were finished and full, Utgard-Loki arrived and escorted them to the outer gate of his castle.

"How will you tell the Gods in Asgard about your contest with my people?" he asked Thor.

"I will tell the shameful truth," Thor replied, "but I will not enjoy it."

"All right," Utgard-Loki said, "but before you leave I will tell you some truths you do not know."

"What?" Thor stopped.

"If I had known your true strength, I would have turned you back at the forest that borders Jotunheim. I have beaten you with magic, not with strength. From the moment you came into my country, you have had us all in fear of your might."

"I do not believe you," Thor said. "Your giant Skrymir thought my hammer-blow was a bird dropping on his cheek!"

Utgard-Loki replied, "It was I you met in the woods, in another guise. I tied the provision bag with iron rods so no ordinary hands could untie it. You thought you had hit *me* three times with your hammer while I slept. Actually I raised a saddle back mountain over my head as you swung Mjollnir, and your hammer sank into the mountain. When you leave, you will see three deep valleys in that mountain, cut by the extraordinary force of your hammer."

Thor's eyes widened, and his heart was lighter. At least his strength was proved once again! But he was awed by the giant-king's powerful magic. "What about the contests?" he asked. "How did you win those so easily?"

"We won no contests," Utgard-Loki said. "In the first, when Loki ate from the trough, his opponent, Logi, was wildfire itself. No man or god can consume meat or bones or wood at the rate of a scorching flame! When your boy Thjalfi ran his three races, Hugi, his opponent, was none other than my own thoughts. No man can travel as fast as a thought!"

"The third contest?" Thor asked. "What was in the horn I drank so lustily out of but could not empty?"

"You did have me worried then," the king admitted. "The other end of the horn was in the sea. Look at the ocean as you return. You will find out how much you drank, for the level has gone down. Already men have a name for this—they call it the ebb tide. It is lucky you did not empty the horn!"

Thor smiled in pleasure, remembering his aching lungs and his deep, deep shame at failing to empty the horn.

The giant went on. "The old woman, Elli, was Old Age herself, and all who have wrestled with her before have fallen dead, not just bent to one knee as you did."

"You forgot the cat," Thor said softly. "What was the cat that I raised nearly to the roof of your castle hall, but could not lift from the floor?"

"Jormungand, the Midgard serpent who lives in the sea and encircles all the earth. If you had lifted that nasty creature one foot higher out of the sea, his venomous breath would have killed all of us instantly!"

Thor started to speak, but the king said sharply, "Now go, and do not come near these gates again. I will not deal so kindly with you next time. You can tell Odin I will use any means to keep my power."

When Thor heard the last threat, he lifted his hammer, whirled around to strike . . . but blinking in the sunlight, he saw only a lovely green field, a large flower-strewn meadow at the foot of a saddleback mountain with three deep chasms cut right through to the plain. But there was no forest, no castle, and no furry, yellow-haired king of the world of giants.

9: THE MANY-HEADED GIANTS

*I have hidden the great
   Thor's hammer
Eight miles down; and back
   again
Shall no man bring it
Till Freyja becomes my wife.*

Odin and Sleipnir were nearly to the end of their long flight home from the Vala's grave, but there were still dark seas, high, ice-covered mountains to cross, and in his mind, years to travel. Odin remembered well the discussion in Asgard when Thor had returned from the east, and then he smiled at the memory of the next of Thor's encounters with the giants.

When Thor and Loki told the Gods about the contests, none were pleased, yet Odin knew they had done their best. Frigga said that Loki should have outwitted the giant because he was a magician. But Thor came to Loki's defense. Utgard-Loki's magic was more powerful and unfathomable than any a God could devise.

"We did frighten the giants," Thor told Odin, "but they would not engage us in any fair battles."

"Why do you always fight?" Balder asked. "You

speak of peace but only search for it with weapons. Not since the war with the Wanes have you settled a quarrel without force."

Tyr said, "The size and power of the giant race makes strength and fierceness the only language we can speak with them."

"My speech was all right," Thor said bitterly. "It was my strength that was lacking!"

Balder persisted, "Men hear of your doings and learn of your battles, your conquests, and your failures. Imitating you, they will fight each other. Where can they look for guidance if their own Gods fail? Why don't you put down your weapons and leave the giants alone. Perhaps then they will leave us in peace."

"The giants are not fair fighters," Thor argued. "They will never leave us alone, nor have they since the beginning of time."

Frigga countered, "I'll wager that if Loki were really one of us, he would have helped Thor, not Utgard-Loki."

"Loki was loyal," Thor answered. "No God can fight fire and win."

Odin interceded in the argument finally, as he so often did. He said, "Thor must continue to show strength. If the giants think we are weak, they will consume the world with fire, sweep it with wind, and flood it with water. I know," Odin said. "I have heard what is written in the runes, and I have looked in the well of all knowledge. I know what I have seen."

"What have you seen in the well?" Bragi asked the Great Creator.

Odin paused. "Reflections," he murmured, then turned back to Thor. "You must fight on," he said.

"Reflections of what?" Bragi persisted, and Frigga leaned toward Odin, listening.

But Odin did not answer. It had always been his way to carry the burdens of his superior knowledge of past and future alone. "Utgard-Loki did not offer peace or treaty," he said to Thor. "His words are my challenge. Go out into the world each day, and wherever and whenever you can, show the strength of the Gods over giants. Do not let their power be unleashed!"

Thor fought on. Daily he challenged any who threatened the freedom or safety of man. He killed nine-headed Thrivaldi, whose thrashings had terrorized an entire fishing village on the northern coasts. He helped Odin betray the giant Suttung who guarded the precious mead of poetry and would let no man taste it. He tracked down and killed, with all of his family, Geirrod, the fire-giant who held birds of the forests captive and threw molten iron across the sky. But each time Thor overcame a giant-enemy, it seemed as if another twice as dangerous needed to be conquered.

One morning Thor woke up and discovered his hammer was missing.

"Sif!" He bellowed so loud the sound raced through all five hundred and forty rooms of his castle. "Where is my hammer?"

His golden-haired wife came quickly. "It is under your bed where you leave it every night," Sif said. "I saw it there myself."

But it was not there. Thor asked every one of his servants, every hero and valkyrie who had been near his home, but no one had seen it and no one knew where to look. Quickly the news spread over Asgard: Thor's hammer was stolen, right from under his bed while he slept! Immediately Frigga came to Bilskirnir and she accused Loki of knowing about it.

"Why do you always blame me?" Loki asked angrily. "I know nothing of Thor's hammer!"

"You are the only one of us who descends from the giant race, and you can hear them plot against us when we hear only wind and rain. You do not belong with us in Asgard!" Frigga said.

"I will ask you to remember that Odin's blood is mixed with mine," Loki said coldly, "and I have as much right to be here as any of you. Do not insult me!"

Balder's son, Forseti, the peacemaker of the Gods, interrupted. "Loki has helped us often enough. We must not be too quick to judge him."

Odin said, "Prove your loyalty by using your knowledge of the giants to find Mjollnir. You will fare no better than we if this weapon is in the hands of an enemy."

"All right," Loki said, "but I hardly know where to look."

Thjalfi spoke up. "Remember when we were in Utgard's hall? A giant with a face like an iceberg sat between us while Thor drank of the sea, and he asked many questions about our mighty giant-battler and his strength, *and* his hammer! Do you remember, Loki?"

Loki's face brightened. "Yes," he said. "Yes, now I remember. That was the master of the frost-giants, whose name is Thrym."

Odin said, "Go down to the north to his realm, and find Thor's hammer!"

Loki said, "Lend me Frigga's hawk feathers so I can fly faster. The disguise will help."

When Loki flew over the world in Frigga's shawl,

the heavens were filled with the sound of whirring wings, and men looked up to see what birds flew northward as they did each spring. Thor waited impatiently for Loki's return.

Loki came back with bad news. He had found Thrym sitting on the top of his black rock mountain, his feet in the valley below. In his hands were eight gold leashes, each clipped to a pet dog as large as a bear. He stroked and smoothed their long-haired backs. Yes, Loki said, Thrym had stolen Mjollnir and buried it eight miles down inside his mountain.

"What will he take to give it back?" Odin asked.

Loki hesitated. "He will accept only one thing."

"What is that? Hurry and tell us," Thor said. "I will give anything!"

"He wants the goddess Freyja for his wife!"

Thor and the others went straight to Folkvang to find Freyja. The beautiful goddess, Njord's daughter, not only was famous for her cat-drawn chariot but for her Brising necklace, the most beautiful and coveted piece of jewelry in Asgard. It had been made for her by some dwarfs out of a collection of tiny rare stones that reflected the light of stars. They were strung on a golden chain so delicately wrought no man could duplicate it. Men worshipped Freyja as the goddess of love, but her own husband had left her years before, and she wept golden tears for him.

When Thor, still furious over the loss of his hammer, told Freyja what Thrym had said, she laughed until she wept more tears of gold. It seemed that every time the Gods bargained with the giants, she was the price they asked! "How ridiculous," she said.

But the Gods were silent.

Freyja looked around the circle of Gods watching

her. She fingered her necklace nervously. Suddenly her dark eyes flashed in anger, and she tossed her head so her black hair flew in Thor's face. She ripped off the Brising necklace and threw it onto the ground.

"Not for all the peace in heaven or earth will I take one step toward the giant's mountain!" she cried. "My gentle father, Njord, gave himself in hostage to the Gods after the war he won. Was it so that the Gods could throw his only daughter to a lustful giant? You will not sell me now or ever to any giant—anywhere!" She climbed into her chariot, called to her cats, and rode high into the sky even as the sun climbed on its way.

Thor looked at Freyr. "Can you bring your sister back? We must persuade her to help us!"

Freyr said no, Freyja's will was her own. "Besides," Freyr added, "she is right. This is not the first time the Gods have risked her life in Asgard bargaining with the giants. We cannot afford to lose our most beautiful goddess of love. There must be some other way you can get your hammer back."

Hermod, the messenger of the Gods, came hurrying into Freyja's hall. He said that Freyja had driven past him and over Bifrost, the rainbow bridge, in such a fury and so fast that he thought she would overtake the sun. What had happened?

Loki explained the problem. Hermod said, "No wonder she was angry." He saw the Brising necklace on the floor and bent to pick it up. "Why doesn't Thor dress as a woman, wear Freyja's necklace, and go down to Thrym's mountain himself?"

"What?" Thor exclaimed. "Me, dress as a woman? Impossible!"

"Be quiet," said Loki. "It's a good idea. Unless

you would rather wait until Thrym rides into Asgard, swinging Mjollnir about his head?"

Odin agreed to the plan, so Sif and Idun helped to dress the big-chested Thor. They put Freyja's Brising necklace on him and gave him a long skirt, a beautifully embroidered vest, a white ruffled blouse, and a pretty cap. Around his waist he wore a golden, jeweled chain that hung to his thighs, and he wore medallions on his chest. Finally they put the prettiest, heaviest bridal veil in Asgard over his face.

Loki put on one of his wife's dresses and went with Thor as the bridesmaid. The two Gods climbed into Thor's chariot, and the impatient goats who pulled it flew to Jotunheim so fast they left a trail of fire.

Thrym saw the chariot from a distance, and as soon as it stopped, he noted the figure wearing the bridal veil. Joyfully he bellowed, "Bestir yourselves, giants! Put straw on the benches, and bring out the beer! Fetch the gold-horned cattle and the jet-black oxen! Bring out my gems and my jewels! Freyja has come to be Thrym's bride! No giant was ever richer than I; the goddess of golden tears was all I lacked and all I craved!"

Hearing this, Thor wanted to tear his dress from his body and meet the greedy giant full strength, but he swallowed his angry words and carefully put out his hand so Thrym could help him down from the chariot. Thrym led his bride to the place of honor at the great feasting table and sat down beside him. The giant's servants brought Thor trays of tiny delicacies, foods fit for a gentle bride. Thor ate every morsel on every tray, and when he had finished all the dainty food, he reached for more. He devoured eight whole salmon and a great black ox. He drank up three gallons of mead and sent the servant who poured it for more.

Loki, who was sitting across the table from Thor and Thrym, saw the giant's mouth open in wonder. Thrym said in amazement, "I never saw a bride who could eat so much or drink so lustily!"

Loki caught Thor's eye, and thinking fast, he disguised his voice as a woman's and said, "Oh, but Freyja has been fasting for eight days and nights, so deep was her longing to be here with you in Jotunheim."

Thrym smiled at that and took a swallow from his horn. Loki sighed in relief. But Thrym leaned over to kiss his bride, and he lifted up the corner of Thor's veil. Thor bristled when that huge, icy face came near his, and Thrym jumped back as though burned.

"Why are my bride's eyes so wild, as if they burn with a furious fire?" Thrym asked.

"Oh, Freyja has not slept in eight lonely nights, so deep was her longing to be your bride," Loki murmured as sweetly as he could.

Again Thrym laughed smugly, while Thor's lungs nearly burst with his desire to breathe free, to deny what Loki said, to shout manfully, to smash this ugly giant who had stolen his hammer. But he glanced at Loki's warning eyes and said nothing at all.

"Now that we have eaten and drunk our fill," Thrym said, "we are ready to take our vows. Sister of mine," he called to a giantess near him, "bring me the rings that belong to Freyja as my wife!"

Not so fast, Thor wanted to say. But cautiously Loki spoke. "Did you not promise to return Thor's hammer to the Gods when Freyja became your bride?"

"Bless me, I did," the giant said, "but now that

I see what a fine big strong woman I have, and how eager she is, I do not think it will be necessary to keep my bargain."

Thor's anger grew mighty, and he clenched his great fists under his shawl when he heard that, but still the giant-killer did not speak.

Loki said in a soft, high voice, "Where have you hidden the famous Mjollnir? How clever you are to have gained two of the Gods' most precious possessions—Thor's hammer and the goddess Freyja, whose necklace alone is worth all your kingdom!"

Thrym thrust out his chest in pride. "The Gods are easily fooled," he said, then turned to his servant. "Bring out Thor's hammer, which will bless our marriage and seal our vows."

Thor saw his precious hammer being carried on a silver cushion by one of Thrym's hideous slaves, and he could contain himself no longer. He said to Thrym as softly and sweetly as he could, "In all the years I have lived among the Gods, I have wanted to touch Thor's hammer, but he has guarded it so jealously— as I have guarded my own Brising necklace—that no one could come near it. Now, as your own bride, do let me hold it for just a moment!"

Thrym blinked in surprise. "Your voice is deep for a woman so fair!"

Quickly Loki said, "For eight days and nights Freyja sang songs of longing and loneliness and love, so impatient was she to come to Jotunheim! Her voice did grow hoarse and husky as a man's."

Thrym grinned again and told his servant to place Mjollnir in the lap of his bride. Thor curled his strong fingers around the short handle of his beloved hammer, gripping the cold, hard metal, and drew his breath deep into his lungs, feeling his whole body fill with strength and joy that was boundless. He waited not one moment longer, but threw back his veil, laughed aloud, leaped onto the table, and brandished his hammer wildly in the air over his head.

Thrym cried out just once before Mjollnir, with all the force of Thor's fury, split his head into a thousand fragments. Then Thor slew all of the company that had gathered on Thrym's mountain for the wedding feast. As he and Loki departed, Thor swung Mjollnir one last time and split the mountain itself wide open, leaving nothing behind but shattered ice and rock.

Triumphantly Thor and Loki took off their women's clothing and climbed back into Thor's chariot to return to Asgard.

As the goats pulled them over the sea, Thor looked below and saw a fleet of men's boats with proudly curved prows being tossed and twisted and buffeted about by high waves and a chopping surf.

Indignantly Thor said to Loki, "See how your overgrown serpent son breaks men's ships and steals the lives of Odin's creations! I will find the Midgard serpent and wrestle with him now!"

When Loki's second child had first come to Asgard with its breath of venom and its tongue of fire, Odin had cast it far out into the sea. But—like the wolf—it grew and grew until its mouth reached its tail. Then it encircled all of Midgard, the land of men.

Thor turned the chariot around, back toward Jotunheim, so suddenly that Loki flew out of the vehicle. He would have fallen into the sea if he had not been wearing his magic shoes with which he could fly. Loki returned to Asgard alone and reported the destruction of the thief of Mjollnir. The Gods rejoiced and prepared a fine feast in celebration. Freyja came back, and when Odin returned her necklace to her, she forgave the Gods and forgot her anger.

Thor, in the meantime, flew until he saw the shore below him, and then he travelled along the beach until he came to the home of a giant named Hymir, who had a boat pulled up on the shore. Thor landed and hid his goats. Pretending to be a young fisherman, he approached the house and knocked on the door.

When it opened, Thor fell back astounded, for the woman who stood there had more heads than he could count, and each one looked at him with a different expression.

One of the heads said, "Who are you who comes to Hymir's house?"

Thor said, "I am only a fisherman, and have heard that Hymir can hook the largest fish in the sea."

Another head said, "True, but my husband is not home. You may come in, but hide from him behind one of those kettles, for he becomes cruel with anger when strangers approach."

Thor saw nine huge kettles, and by the smell he knew they contained wine of a very fine sort. He thought how Odin would like to taste this wine. He hid himself behind one and waited for the giant's return. It was a long wait, and Thor fell asleep. Suddenly he was wakened by a blast of cold air and the slamming of a door. He peered around the vat and saw a giant in the doorway. His bulk filled the whole side of the room, and his black hip-boots were as tall as Thor himself. Hymir rubbed his hands, which were blue with cold. His beard was so covered with icicles it looked like a forest of frozen trees, and his hair was a mountain of snow.

"Who has come while I've been gone?" he said in a rasping voice to his multi-headed wife.

The giantess fluttered about him, her heads smiling at him from many angles. "Just a young lad who wants to go fishing with you," she said.

Hymir grumbled, "Well, where is he?" The giant stared across the room so fiercely that eight of the nine kettles fell to pieces and wine flowed over the floor. Thor stepped out from behind the ninth.

"I have heard that you catch the greatest fish in the sea," said Thor. "I have wanted to see how you do it. Will you go fishing with me?"

Hymir grunted at the God and did not answer right away. He frowned and blew on his hands and finally said, "Well, all right. But you must find your own bait. I will not give you mine."

Thor went outside and in a field nearby saw a herd of black oxen. He killed one and took the head with him. He met Hymir at the long boat.

"I have my bait," he said to the giant, who looked askance at the ox head dripping blood. "Are you ready?"

Hymir began to push the boat into the water. "All right," he grumbled, "but you have to row. Do you think you're strong enough to handle my boat?"

Thor said he thought he was strong enough, and took up the oars. When they were well offshore, Hymir dropped his lines into the sea and told Thor he could stop rowing.

"No," said Thor, "I want to go farther out."

Hymir was silent, but suddenly the boat twisted around and Thor knew there was something on Hymir's line. The giant reeled in a whale with ease, took the hook out of its gaping mouth, and tied the whale to the back of the long boat. Hymir dropped his lines back into the water and told Thor not to row out any more, that this was far enough.

"No," said Thor, "I want to go farther out." He pulled harder on the oars, for now he was dragging Hymir's whale. Again something tugged on the giant's line, and the giant reeled in another whale, stunned it with a blow, and tied it with the first to the back of the boat. Again he told Thor to stop; they had gone out to sea far enough.

Thor said, "No, I want to go farther," and continued to row, now pulling both whales behind him. Hymir's frown grew deeper, and as Thor rowed farther and farther from shore, he looked more worried.

Finally the giant stood up in the boat. "Stop!" he shouted, "I order you to stop or we will be in the territory of the Midgard serpent, and he will pull us to the bottom of the sea!"

Thor threw back his head and laughed heartily. "That is where I hoped to be," he said to Hymir. He put down his oars and threw his hook and line with the ox head on it over the side of the boat. Hymir's eyes grew large with fear, and his fists were tightly clenched. Thor was scornful of how frightened the braggart giant really was! There was a sudden hard tug on Thor's line, and giant and God were thrown against the side of the boat. Where moments before the sea had been calm, now it foamed and churned, and waves rose and broke around them. Thor grabbed his line and pulled on it as hard as he could, letting it fall any which way in the bottom of the boat.

Hymir shouted at him, "Let it go! Let it go!" But the great god Thor reeled in, knowing that at last he would have his chance to conquer the serpent that encircled the earth. He kept Mjollnir tight in his belt, and his gloves were well on. The stern of the boat went down, and the curved prow rose, and then the right gunwale dipped into the sea, and water flowed in. Thor placed one foot on each side of the boat, pulling with all his strength on the taut line that tore at his hands. Suddenly in front of his face a dragon's head rose, so wild and fierce that even in his most elaborate visions he had not dreamed what it would be. The eyes were fireballs, and the tongue was flame, and the orange teeth were jagged. Held in the jaw that was covered with foam was the black ox head, and the hook that Thor had hidden in it protruded from the top of the monstrous skull.

The beast put two clawed feet on the gunwale, and Thor raised his hammer high, taking careful aim. He knew that the breath of the serpent was lethal. Just as he swung toward the center of the ugly skull, Hymir, who had been cowering in terror against the side of the boat, reached out and cut Thor's line. The dragon slipped back under the surface as Mjollnir flew. The water turned red and bubbled with blood. Thor knew his hammer had hit the serpent, but he could not be sure it was dead, for Mjollnir lost power when it went through water, and Thor did not see the dragon die.

Angry at being robbed of his prey, the great god Thor lifted Hymir in his two strong hands and threw him from the boat into the thrashing sea. Thor's own feet broke through the bottom of the boat, and water filled the hull. Thor called his hammer back and waded to shore.

Hymir's many-headed wife met him on the strand, and every head jabbered at Thor with the same question: "Where is my husband? What have you done to Hymir?"

Thor said, "He is with the serpent at the bottom

10: THREATS

The fate of all does Frigga know well
Though herself she says it not.

All the long, windy night Heimdall paced the rainbow bridge, impatiently waiting for Odin and Sleipnir to ride back from the gates of Niflheim with messages from the wise woman of the dead. Heimdall had promised to alert Frigga and the others as soon as he heard Sleipnir's hooves. He listened hard. In the distance he heard the heroes still carousing in Valhalla, and once during the night he thought he heard a dog howl, but it could have been only the wind.

Heimdall was well suited to his post as keeper of Bifrost, the rainbow bridge, and guard of Asgard. His ears were so sensitive he could hear both the grass and the wool on a sheep's back grow. He could see for a hundred miles by day or by night, and he needed less sleep than a bird. Heimdall had a horn—the Gjaller-horn—with which he would warn the Gods if danger approached, but he kept it well hidden under the root of Yggdrasil by Urd's well.

There was frost in the air, and Heimdall knew that already some of the high lakes in Midgard would be frozen over. The mists blew around him so that sometimes the golden bricks which paved the bridge seemed silver, and sometimes they disappeared altogether. He walked nearly to the end of the bridge. When he turned he saw a tall woman's figure, shrouded in mist at the Asgard end. He ran quickly toward her, wondering how anyone could have gotten past him. But it was only Frigga, miserably holding her hawk feathers around her.

"What are you doing out in the cold tonight?" he asked her.

"I could not sleep. Those heroes are wilder than ever," she said. "I could not hear Sleipnir's gallop, nor your horn either, for the sound of their laughter."

"I told you I would call you," Heimdall said gently. "By the nine maidens who were my mother, you know I keep my word!"

Frigga shivered and was silent a moment. Finally she said, "Forseti and Hoder went on to Breidablik, and Idun and Bragi went home. Thor and Sif wait with Tyr and Freya and Freyja, down in Folkvang, and Njord sings his songs by the sea. I sat in Odin's tower, and I could only see a little distance into the courtyard below. He has greater vision with one eye than all of us do with our two. I thought of the last time he went riding off in search of the mead of poetry and I waited here with you for his return. Remember?"

Heimdall nodded. "I remember."

"He flew in with a giant hot behind him then, so it was good that we waited and could give early warning of his approach." She paused. "Tonight I did not want to be alone. Do you mind if I wait with you?"

"No," the guardian of the Gods said quietly. "I do not mind."

They were silent awhile, and Heimdall turned his head this way and that to catch any sound or motion in the air. The wind was cold and whistled around the rocky mountaintops below them, and now and then the scent of burning peat and sheepdung blew in from Midgard.

Heimdall said, "I suppose now it is cold enough below so that men will keep their fires going nearly all the time."

Frigga said, "I have seen their little houses with the roof holes above the firepits. It is a wonder that men can see at all by the time spring comes, for the smoke that fills their rooms."

"Now that the nights are long, perhaps they will stay home peacefully for a while, leaving their wars until another spring," Heimdall said.

"With all that Odin made of them and for them," Frigga murmured, "why should they be at war? What greeds and hungers fill their minds, so that my son's sleep is torn?"

"I can see a long, long way," Heimdall told her, "but I cannot see into men's hearts, nor into the past or future. I cannot see truth or wisdom, only danger when it looms up in a giant's form." He sighed. "Each of us is here for some special purpose. But the kind of knowledge you seek, you will have to get from someone else. I can only wait and watch and warn."

Frigga pulled her shawl around her. "I think what you say is true. I wish Odin would hurry back."

It was nearly dawn of the second night when Heimdall suddenly said, "Listen!"

"I hear nothing," Frigga said. "Only the beating of my worried heart."

"You will in a moment," the guard said. Hardly

had he spoken when Sleipnir, with all eight legs flying, came racing across the rainbow bridge. Odin drew his horse to a halt beside Frigga and Heimdall, and climbed down from Sleipnir's back.

"What have you heard and what have you learned?" Frigga asked anxiously.

"What did the dead wise woman say?" Heimdall asked.

Odin pushed back his hood, laid a gentle hand on Frigga's shoulder, and said, "Behind Hel's tall gates there are preparations for a festival."

Frigga drew in her breath short. "Whom do they expect?"

"Balder."

Frigga's hand flew to her mouth, and for a moment no one said anything.

Heimdall reached down and brought out the great golden Gjaller-horn and put it to his lips. He would have blown it, but Odin's hand stopped him.

"Wait," the All-Father said. "Do not blow the Gjaller-horn now."

"Why not?" Heimdall said angrily. "If Balder's life is threatened, all the Gods should know to come to his defense! We will fight off any enemy of our best god!"

"What do you mean?" Frigga asked, finding her voice at last. "What did the Vala say?"

Odin hesitated. During the long night's ride he had pondered how to tell Frigga what he had heard. He had thought of the contrast between Balder, smiling always, bringing laughter and sunlight wherever he went, and Hoder, blind, quiet, and sometimes disturbingly wise. He had asked himself what that dark world was really like. Could Hoder possibly harbor such anger and jealously that he would rise up wrathfully against the brother he seemed to adore? Would Frigga—learning of the prophecy—cast out the blind son to protect the beautiful one she loved so much? Odin looked at his sons' mother, saw the pain of fear in her dark eyes, and knew that he had to share his knowledge with her. He had to trust her to believe as he did—that there was something still not revealed in the Vala's prophecy. Perhaps Frigga, always a skeptic, but always believing in the worthiness of her sons, would be better able to perceive the truth than he.

"The Vala said that Hoder would wield the weapon of death," the oldest god said to his wife.

Heimdall said in surprise, "Hoder?"

"Hoder?" Frigga echoed. Then as if thinking out loud she said, "I have two sons of Odin's, and I love them with my life. I have seen how they love each other, though one is joyful as the other is sad." She walked away from Odin and Heimdall, and looked across the lightening sky. To Odin her figure suddenly seemed frail and unlike herself. He went quietly to her side and put his arm around her shoulders.

Frigga did not pull away, but continued, "Every time a child of man is born, it is as if Balder, too, were born again. For every infant at birth is pure and untouched by the world's hard ways. As he grows, a man can be blinded by the darkness of the night, or by the smoke from his own fire, or by the admission of evil into his heart. But evil cannot enter our Balder's heart, and even the pinprick of a star's flickering light can never penetrate Hoder's dark world. Yet Hoder speaks only of love." Suddenly, as if gaining new strength, Frigga turned to Odin and said, "All of us have waited for the wisdom of the dead, but now I think that the dead woman of hell may not be wise."

Odin smiled. Now Frigga sounded like her old, strong self again. "Come," he said, "let us go and tell the others."

"But do not tell them about Hoder!" Frigga said. "They might not understand as we do."

When the other Gods heard that Balder's life was in danger, they reacted with quick fury. "I'll smash any giant who comes near Balder," Thor bellowed, waving Mjollnir about his head so wildly that his servants ran out of his range. "If Balder dies, the Midgard serpent can rise again from the sea-bottom where I left him!"

"If Balder dies," Idun said, "the leaves on my apple tree will wither and fall, and in the spring no flowers will grow on it, and no fruit. Then all of us will grow old and die."

Freyja mused, "There's a meadow high in the Midgard hills where I like to go each spring, and sometimes lovers go there too." She paused as if waiting for a memory. "When the sun has warmed the western slope, it becomes covered with tiny yellow flowers, and it looks as if the whole hill were made of gold. By summer the grass is a soft green carpet where sheep graze and grow fat. If Balder dies, there will be no lovers, and no spring." The goddess bit her lip, and two red-gold tears rolled down her smooth cheeks.

"I lost my hand to chain the wolf so that men and Gods could be free and safe," Tyr said. "But if Balder dies, I'll need my hand to battle the Fenris Wolf, for Gleipnir will break when the good god perishes."

Bragi spoke of a field where children ride their ponies and the white-winged ptarmigans fly out of their nests in the brush as the hoofs gallop by. And Sif remembered a frozen lake that in winter was an icy prison between high stone cliffs, but in spring was like a crystal jewel in the mountains where swans gathered and small birds sang.

"If Balder dies, no pond will thaw, no bird will dare to nest, no pony will run on a sunny field. Even the fish will stay in the depths of the sea, for the whole world will remain in darkness, and spring will not come," Bragi said sadly.

"No spring!" The heroes and valkyries began to talk at once. Odin and Frigga stood among the Gods and Goddesses, listening to their fears, their angry words. Odin watched Frigga, and saw how the look on her face changed. She said nothing now, no tears came to her eyes, no words escaped her lips. But she began to frown, listening to the clamor in the court, and he saw her lips tighten.

Suddenly she turned to Odin and said indignantly, "They're like a bunch of gabbling children! All they talk about is what they'll lose, yet not one of them has thought of doing anything useful! Who has gone to Balder and Nanna and promised to protect them? Nobody! It is up to me," she said, her eyes flashing. "I will take Balder's destiny into my own hands."

"What will you do?" Odin asked.

"I will defy the so-called wise woman. All things in the world trust me. I will see which is stronger, the Vala's words or my will."

Frigga swept out of the courtyard. She went to her home, Fensalir, where she ordered her servant to prepare for a journey.

11: PROMISES

Charms full good then cha...
to me, mother,
And seek thy son to guard.

Within the hour Frigga's servant, Gna, had saddled the swift horse, Hofvarpnir, which could go through air and over water. The goddesses rode onto the plains, where great black rock pillars stood bare to the sun and the wind. Frigga dismounted and, putting hands on her hips, called to the rocks.

"Do you love Balder as all the world does?"

The rocks answered from all around her, "Yes."

"Will you promise not to harm him, neither to fall upon him nor to stand in his way when he walks, nor to allow your sharp edges to break his skin? Will you promise for yourselves and for all rocks for all time?"

The rocks said yes, they would not harm Balder. And they promised for themselves and their kin for all time.

Then Frigga and Gna rode Hofvarpnir to the edge of the world, where waves from all seas broke on the shore and the foam spread over their feet and clutched at their ankles. Frigga spoke loud to the waves as they crashed on the sand, and she asked them, "Does water love Balder as all the world does?"

The waves slipped away and then rose up again, saying, "Yes!"

"Will you promise not to harm him, not to drag him to your depths, nor fill his lungs, nor carry him on your currents, nor freeze him, nor crush him in your great blocks of ice that float down from the north?"

The ocean became calm and the waves gentle, and water said yes, it would promise to protect Balder and do him no harm.

Frigga and Gna rode to the rim of a pit from which they could see into the furnace of the fire world, and Frigga spoke to the flames. The flames said yes, fire would not harm Balder, neither burn him nor consume the air he might breathe.

Frigga and Gna rode into the forest, and Frigga spoke to the trees. She said, "Will you promise to protect Balder for now and all time? Not to fall on him should lightning split your trunk; not to let him go if he climbs into your arms; not to poison him with the juice of your leaves or sap; not to touch him with a weapon of wood?"

The trees swayed and shook their leaves and said, "If Balder dies, there will be no forests, for the Fimbul winter will kill us. We will promise to protect Balder and let no wooden weapon harm him."

Frigga took oaths from all the elements, from metals and crystals and from the air itself. She talked to all growing things on the earth, flowers and shrubs, grasses and lichens, molds and mosses. She spoke with all animals, beasts and birds and insects and

creatures of the sea. Everyone vowed not to harm Balder. Frigga spoke with those spirits who cause sickness among men, and hunger and sorrow and despair. All promised to stay far from Balder and do him no harm.

"Come now," Frigga said to Gna with a sigh. "Balder is safe. We can go home to Asgard."

They hurried through the western woods, for it was nearly dark. Once Gna called to Frigga and pointed to the old, gnarled trunk of a great oak tree. "Look, there's a little low branch on that tree, growing out of a knot, and the leaves do not seem to be quite the same as the oak's. Do you suppose we should take an oath from it too?"

Frigga glanced at the tiny shoot, growing like a sucker from the old bark. She was tired, and she was impatient to be home. She said, "That is only a tiny mistletoe, a parasite of a plant with no strength of its own, nor will even to give a promise. Besides," she added, "it is much too young and slender and weak to do any harm." Frigga spurred Hofvarpnir on. "Come," she said, "we have done all we need."

The Gods were just gathering for the evening feast when Frigga and Gna returned and told them what they had done.

"You mean," Tyr asked, "that if I threw a stone at Balder, it could not harm him because rocks have given you their oath?"

"That is *exactly* what I mean," Frigga said proudly. "Try it."

Balder stood against the wall, and Tyr picked up a large, rough stone. Nanna ran to Balder and put her arms around him, crying, "No, Tyr, No!" But Balder put his finger to her lips and gently moved her away. "Hush, Nanna," he said. "You musn't be afraid. If Tyr's rock hurts me, then the rocks will have lied to Frigga. If the rocks lied, then all things might lie, and I would be better off dead. But if the rock does not harm me or break my skin, then we shall know that Frigga's will is strong, that truth can win over falsehood, and good can overcome evil. So let Tyr throw his stone and aim for my heart or my head. Let fly!"

Tyr hurled the stone. The Gods and Goddesses drew in their breath. The stone flew straight and true toward Balder's smooth brow. Nanna covered her eyes. Frigga watched with chin held high. Not six inches away from Balder's eyes the stone stopped, then dropped straight to the ground at his feet.

The crowd roared. Balder broke into a laugh of joy that rippled and echoed over all the dwellings in Asgard, and everyone in heaven and on earth heard him laugh and joined him.

Suddenly Thor picked up a spear that one of the heroes had left lying around, and sent it toward Balder. That, too, dropped to the ground, as if there were an impenetrable, invisible wall around Balder.

The happy news spread like the wind. The feast in Valhalla that night had never been more joyous. Everywhere men and Gods, heroes and Goddesses, laughed and kissed and said to each other, "Balder is safe! The Gods are safe! The world is safe! Spring will come again next year!"

12: THJAZI'S EYES

And I hurled the eyes of the
  giant's son
To the hot heavens above.
These marks are the
  mightiest of all my deeds
That men have ever seen.

Odin stood in his tower watching the game in the courtyard below, listening to the raucous laughter that echoed up to his private window. He glanced at Frigga, who was looking at Balder. She was so pleased with herself, admiring her handsome son, all in white, alive as ever with his fair hair blowing in the cool breeze. Balder's laughter brightened all the hours as the Gods and heroes bombarded him with missiles of every kind. Each time a stone or a lance hurtled his way, he pretended to be frightened, holding his hand to his head or his heart, and no one tired of the suspense. Then, as the weapons fell to the ground, everyone laughed as if it were the first stone again. It seemed that the Gods and heroes were like little children.

"Do you think they will ever grow tired of the game?" Frigga asked, cutting into Odin's thoughts. He frowned. On the breeze was the smell of smoke.

In Midgard, men would be asking Njord to temper the fires, keep the seas calm, and protect their homes for the winter ahead. But when smoke rose from the south, it was usually not men's fires, but Surt's, reaching up from Muspellheim's furnaces, and something was amiss. There were strange rumblings within the earth, and once Odin's tower trembled.

Odin was still apprehensive. Wisest of all, he sensed that something was wrong, something was missing. Nothing was without meaning, he thought, not even a breeze. Nothing was without effect, even the swords that lay so innocently on the ground. Each word, each sound, each flapping of an eagle's wing as it flew, was part of a grand design, moving toward a certain end.

Odin glanced up to the sky, and even though it was morning, Thjazi's star-eyes seemed to be winking at him, warning him, laughing at him. Those two stars were the first to appear each evening and the last to disappear after the sunrise. This was not the first time Odin wished the Gods had not killed Thjazi, but would it be the last? He nodded to those mocking stars and remembered how they came to be there.

Odin, the timid Hoenir, and Loki had become lost one day among the rocky, barren hills of Midgard. For days they had wandered, seeing no growing grain to eat, not a berry nor a piece of meat, just miles of rubble and black rock. Though Odin had no need of food, Loki and Hoenir were starved. Finally they saw a forest on another hill and a herd of oxen grazing in a green field at its edge. Hoenir and Odin killed one of the beasts and hung it on a spit to roast over a fire. The meat sizzled and browned, and Loki's and Hoenir's mouths watered at the marvelous aroma of the freshly roasted flesh. They could hardly wait to taste it. But when Hoenir bit into the first piece, it was quite raw.

Loki put the meat back on the fire. After what seemed long enough, and when he could stand the tantalizing smell no longer, Loki bit into a piece of meat. It still was raw.

Odin was suspicious. They must have crossed into a land where they were in the power of a giant, he thought. A rustling in the tree above his head made him look up. An eagle as tall as an old pine tree sat on the hilltop above them, flapping its wings and laughing.

"What do you know of the ox we have slain?" Odin asked the eagle.

"I know that unless you give me my share, it will never be cooked," the eagle replied.

Hoenir, who was fanning the fire, said nervously, "What shall we do?"

Odin answered, "We had better offer him a share." Turning back to the eagle, he said, "Cook it for us, and you shall have some of the meat."

As soon as the eagle-giant sat by the fire, the meat was tender. The huge bird picked up one ox thigh in one talon, and the other thigh in his other talon, and began to tear the delicious meat from the whole cooked beast.

Loki cried out in a shrill voice, "Save some for us! You can't have it all!" The eagle merely turned his feathered back on Loki and continued to eat. Loki was so angry he grabbed the spit and drove it hard into the breast of the eagle. There it stuck. But the big bird slowly stretched its wide wings and rose from the ground in a slow circle. The other end of the pole stuck hard to Loki's hands, so that he could not let go. "Oh!" he cried, but the eagle dragged him over rock and rubble, thorn and brush, bumping and bruising him so he screamed with pain and fright. His knees were raw and his arms nearly pulled out of their sockets.

"Help! Save me!" he screamed, but soon was so far away that his words were like mere rattling stones. The eagle flew up and over the sea into Jotunheim, the land of the giants. Then he dropped to the ground.

Loki lay panting, but still stuck fast to the spit. When he could breathe again, he said, "Who are you, and what must I give you to let me go?"

The eagle glanced at Loki, bleeding and sore, then studied its greasy talons casually. Finally it said, "I am Thjazi, and Thrymheim is my home. Bring me Bragi's wife, and I will set you free."

Loki trembled. Of all the Goddesses in Asgard, Idun was the favorite, for the apples that grew from her tree nourished the Gods and kept them from growing old.

"Not Idun," Loki said to Thjazi. "The Gods would never let her go! What else will you take?"

Thjazi flapped his wings and prepared to rise. "Idun is all I want and all I'll take. I have a lovely daughter, Skadi is her name, and I would like to see her stay so young and lovely forever!"

"I'll give you anything else," Loki said, "but Bragi never lets Idun leave his side, he loves her so. I'll give you gold; I'll bring you magic weapons from the dwarfs. But I'll never get Idun to come to Thrymheim."

The eagle spoke no more but rose straight into the air, and Loki crashed into a tree as he swung along behind. "Stop," he cried out. "Stop! I'll do it! Somehow I will bring Idun to you. I promise. . . ."

When Odin and Hoenir returned to Asgard they did not tell anyone of their encounter with Thjazi. Loki came back a few days later beaten and sore, and told no one how he had managed to escape. He hung about the Gods, watching Idun and Bragi, waiting for a chance to talk with the keeper of the golden apples alone. It was not easy, for the wise old poet adored his wife and did not like to let her go far away from him even for short times.

One evening, however, Odin called the high Gods to Gladsheim for a council meeting to discuss Thor's recent contest with the giants. While Bragi was listening to Odin's problems, Loki found Idun sitting alone by Urd's fountain, pensive and lovely.

"May I have one of your apples?" the wily one asked her.

Idun was startled. "I did not know you were in Asgard," she said. "Why aren't you with the others at Gladsheim?"

"No one invited me," Loki replied. "Odin does not often let me join the Gods in council, though why I do not know. I know a lot about the giants that would be helpful." He paused a moment and then softly said, "And I know where there is a tree loaded with apples as good—or better—than yours!"

Idun sat up straight. "Nonsense," she said sharply. "That cannot be true. There are no other apples like mine." She thought for a moment. "These days my supply does run short, though. There have been so many battles among men, and so many new heroes come to Valhalla, sometimes I . . ."

"The tree I saw was laden," Loki said quickly, "and its golden apples were larger than yours. Sweeter too," he added.

"I don't believe you," Idun said angrily. But with

her finger drew an outline of an apple on the sandy soil. Loki watched her carefully.

Finally the best-loved goddess said, "But you know, I could use some more, just in case . . ."

"In case of what?"

Idun did not answer right away. How could she admit to Loki that she was afraid the Gods would not love her so well if she ran out of apples? And what would happen to them if her tree stopped bearing fruit? Yet, Loki had lied to the Gods before, she knew. She studied his delicately beautiful face, and sighed. "Where did you see the tree?"

"In the western woods," Loki said, "quite near the bridge, really. Ask Odin. He and I were there together just the other day. That little tree's branches nearly touched the ground, the fruit was so heavy."

"Show me," Idun said suddenly and stood up. Loki took her hand and led her toward the forest. Once in the shadows of the trees, he let her go and ran ahead.

"Wait," the goddess called. "Wait for me."

"Follow me," Loki shouted to her. "I'll show you the way." When they were deeper into the woods, he ran a bit faster, and Idun had to turn this way and that to follow him.

"Slow down," she called again, panting. "I can't keep up with you." But Loki darted in and out of the trees faster and faster. Suddenly Idun did not know which way he had gone. She ran and ran quite alone until she fell exhausted on the needle-covered roots of a spreading spruce tree. She put her head down and wept, half hoping Loki would come back and find her, and half hoping he would leave her alone so she wouldn't have to run any more. Finally she sat up, rubbed her sore eyes, and wondered if there ever had been another apple tree. If only she could be home with Bragi right now, instead of lost and alone in this darkening forest! She nearly began to cry again.

"Loki?" she called to the wily one.

There was no answer.

"Loki?" she called again, a little louder. There was a rustling in the trees, but no answer. She wondered which way to start to find her way home, but it was suddenly so dark that even the trunks of the trees were hard to see. She tried to see in which direction the sun had set, but just as she looked up, she heard a great flapping around her. A wild wind blew her hair and dress about, and then she felt herself clutched in the sharp claws of an enormous bird and swept through the branches of the trees high into the air. Sick and dizzy, she saw the tree-tops wobble and grow small beneath her. She couldn't breathe. She was dying! She knew she would never see Asgard or Bragi again. She fainted in the eagle's claws, and her tears fell into the sea.

It was early morning when Balder, on his way to Midgard, found Bragi the poet on the rainbow bridge, scanning the clouds and hills of the worlds below. Tears ran down his wrinkled cheeks into his soft beard.

"What is the matter, old man?" Balder asked.

Bragi wet his lips and tried to speak, but his voice did not work.

"What is it?" Balder asked Heimdall, who was looking as far as he could into the distance.

"Idun is gone," Heimdall answered, without turning around.

"What do you mean, gone?"

"Vanished, stolen, disappeared, dead. Just gone. No one knows where. Bragi said she did not come home last night, and no one has seen her this morning."

Balder was silent a moment, a clouded thought forming in his mind, as if he were remembering a place he had been long ago, or perhaps dreamed.

"And you, Heimdall, you have seen no trace of Idun? No giants approached yesterday or today?"

"No," Heimdall said, "no giants. No Idun."

"We must tell Odin at once," Balder said. "He will know how and where to find her."

But Odin, too, was at a loss. He sent his ravens to look for Idun, and he searched with his far-seeing eye over the world, but for days and then weeks there was no sign of the sweet goddess. Bragi's silence deepened. At the evening feasts he sang no songs and told no tales of heroism to lighten the spirits of the Gods. Conquest after conquest went unheralded.

One night Frigga looked down the length of the table in Valhalla and said to Odin, "Look at Sif."

Odin studied Thor's wife, whose hair of spun gold reached nearly to her waist. The skin on her neck was wrinkled, and there were deep gray pockets below her eyes. Startled, he looked at Thor, whose energy was boundless though he was the first son. Odin saw Thor's big hand tremble as he picked up his horn of mead, and the purple veins stood out on the loose skin of his hand.

"They're growing old," Odin said and looked hard at Frigga's time-worn face.

"Without Idun's apples we will all grow old and withered," Frigga said. "You must do something to find her."

Odin nodded. Just then he saw Loki come into the hall to join the feast, late, as he often was. He stood hesitantly under the wolf by the western door and glanced nervously at the empty seat beside Bragi's place. Odin understood.

His words resounded through the length and breadth of the stone vaulted hall. "Half-brother and doer of evil, son of giants and father of wolves, what have you done with the goddess Idun?"

Loki looked up as if caught suddenly in a shaft of light. "No-nothing," he stammered.

"Liar!" The Gods spoke as one voice; their roar was heard like thunder over the heavens. Thor pulled on his gauntlets and reached for his hammer. Tyr grabbed one of Loki's arms, Forseti the other, and they held him tight while Odin and Thor approached.

Thor raised his hammer over Loki's head, but Odin held Thor's arm and said, "Do not kill him. First he must tell us where Idun is. Then we can punish him."

Shaking with fear, Loki told Odin of his pact with Thjazi. "I didn't want to give her to the giant," he said. "I, too, am growing old without her. I only wanted to be free."

"Why did you not tell us right away where she was?" Odin asked.

"I was afraid," Loki said. "I knew you would be angry, and besides, you had no power over Thjazi either. He tricked us all!"

Odin thought for a moment. Finally he said, "Well, bring Idun back to Asgard and we will forgive you and forsake any punishment. But you must get her safely inside the gates!"

Loki sighed in relief and once again asked to borrow Frigga's shawl. "I will return with Idun," he promised the Gods.

Frigga took off her feathers and gave them to Loki. Once again the skies whirred with the sound of his flight as he flew to Jotunheim. On the mountaintop,

Thrymheim, he found Thjazi's castle, and all night long crouched in wait by the gate. In the morning he saw the huge eagle rise in flight and go off over the hills. Cautiously Loki slipped through the gate and went across the yard. Still in the guise of the hawk, he flew to window after window, hoping for sight or sound of Idun. Suddenly he heard a woman weeping. The distant sound came from the top of the tower at the corner of the castle overlooking the sea. He flew to the window and peered into a cold stone room. There in the corner was Idun, wrinkled and thin, huddled miserably against the wall.

"Come," he whispered to her from the sill where he perched. She looked up at the sound, and at first did not connect his voice with the small falcon perched there. "Come here!" Loki said again.

Idun rose and went to the window cautiously, curiously. When she was close enough for him to touch, Loki reached out a claw and grabbed her arm. "Ow!" she cried, but immediately he changed her into a walnut. Tightly clutching the nut in his claw, he flew straight out over the sea toward Asgard.

The Gods stood on the wall anxiously waiting for Loki's return. They cheered when they saw the hawk fly toward them, but suddenly in the sky behind they saw a huge eagle in pursuit. Thjazi had returned and found Idun gone. Seeing the hawk in the distance, he had flown after it. The eagle's wingspread was many times that of the hawk, and the giant gained on Loki so fast that the Gods thought he would be caught.

They rushed outside the walls of Asgard and lit a bonfire. The hawk flew through the flames, singeing its wings, and dropped its precious walnut safely inside by Bragi's feet. Bragi looked at the little brown nut on the ground and touched it gently with his toe. Immediately Idun stood beside him and fell into his arms.

"Bless you, bless you," the old man cried, and this time the tears that ran into his beard were tears of happiness.

Meanwhile the Gods outside had fanned the fire, making the flames leap higher than ever. Thjazi tried to stop from flying through but his speed was too great. His wings caught fire, and he fell to the ground. Thor strode out of the gates and let Mjollnir fly, and Thjazi lay dead beside the wall.

Odin looked down at the dead giant, the same eagle who had stolen first their meat and then their goddess of youth. But Thjazi might never have harmed the Gods, Odin knew, if they had stayed home. Odin took Thjazi's eyes and threw them to the sky, where they stuck and stayed, two stars, forever. After that, those stars often seemed to watch him, like a conscience from above, and say things to him that he did not always understand, just as the eye he had given to Mimir sometimes seemed to watch him from the world below.

Were Thjazi's eyes watching this game in the courtyard now? Odin wondered. How confident the Gods were of Balder's safety! Did those star eyes see something that Odin had missed? He watched Forseti tap Hoder on the shoulder and say a word to him, perhaps asking him to join the fun. Hoder shook his head no, but Forseti picked up a heavy stone and threw it at his shining father. Balder laughed and caught it harmlessly in his palm. The heroes laughed. Frigga smiled. Hoder turned away from the sound and stood quietly in a doorway alone. Thjazi's eyes flickered at Odin, pricking his mind. All the Gods but Hoder joined the game, Odin thought . . . all the Gods but . . .

Suddenly he knew what was wrong. Hoder was not the only one left out! *Loki* was as separate from this game of life and death as was Balder's blind brother!

How stupid he had been to forget Loki, Odin thought. The Vala was wrong. It would not be blind Hoder who would threaten Balder, but the one who always caused trouble, the sly deceiver, the half-brother he never wanted, Loki! He looked up to those stars once again. It had been Thjazi's eyes, reminding him of Loki's past treachery, that had made him see the true danger. He hoped it was not too late.

Odin clapped his hands, and Hugin and Munin flew to him and sat on his shoulders. "Fly out over the world," he said to his ravens. "Find Loki. Do not tell him I sent you, but see what he is doing and report back to me." When the big black birds flew over the yard, their shadows travelled across Balder's figure, and Nanna and Bragi looked up.

Frigga shivered and pulled her shawl around her. "Why are you looking for Loki?" she asked.

"I am not sure," Odin said.

13: LOKI WAGERS
HIS HEAD

*In the days of old Ivaldi's
sons did
Fashion Skidbladnir fair;
It was the best of ships
For the bright god Freyr ...*

It always bothered the Gods that Loki had to live among them in Asgard. He was the son of two giants, Laufey and Farbauti. In the morning of time, when the Gods were first born, Odin had adopted Loki as his brother, but no one knew just how or why, and Odin did not explain.

Greedy, jealous, sly, but also intelligent, beautiful, and so talented in magic that he could turn himself into almost any kind of man or beast or bird, Loki had often seemed to be the source of trouble among the Gods. Just as often he seemed to cause others to do wrong. But though the Gods often regretted it, they had to accept Loki as one of them, for good and for evil. He had been devious, mischievous, and treacherous, and his three children—the Fenris Wolf, the Midgard serpent, and the hag Hel, to whom Odin had given Niflheim, land of the dead, for her domain—were feared by all. But Loki had also given the Gods their most precious possessions.

The strange mixture of good and bad had alway been Loki's way and Loki's mystery. If God or ma had an evil thought, Loki expressed it. If a God ha a jealous bent, Loki played on it.

Back in time when Asgard was young and th Gods had not known how to fight the giants, Lo had sat by a clump of yew trees watching Thor wife, Sif, reading by a river. The mischief-mak looked longingly at her thick yellow hair, flowin like a shining liquid over her smooth back. He seethe with a primitive jealousy. *His* wife, Sigyn, had ha that no man would remember. Wouldn't she like t have golden strands like those! Why had the Grea Creator given so much to Thor and so little to hin

Loki slipped over behind Sif and cut off all tho silk strands. Sif felt the snips too late. She jumpe and cried out in misery when she saw her beautif hair in Loki's hands. Then Sif ran all the way t Bilskirnir, Thor's hall, through its many rooms unt she found her husband, the mighty first son of Odi

"Look what Loki has done to me!" she cried an threw herself weeping into his arms.

Thor's roar of anger reverberated from all the hill and Loki, hearing thunderous threats, ran away fro Asgard as fast as he could.

Thor chased Loki all the way to the rainbow bridg There he caught him, dragged him back into Odin court, and held him over a stone, threatening to brea his neck.

"Wait," Loki cried, "don't kill me! I will get S some new hair, better than her old!" Desperately h promised, "I will go to the dwarfs and have the make her some hair of pure gold."

Thor paused, but did not let Loki loose. He aske Odin. "What shall I do with the wretch?"

Odin said, "Do not kill him. Loki should be tried and punished by the court of high Gods. But," the All-Father added, "the court might be lenient if he atones for his sins." He then ordered Loki to go to the dwarfs and get new hair for Sif—also to bring back some weapons that would help the Gods defend themselves against the giants' attacks.

Thor let Loki go, and the jealous God flew down to the land under the mountains, where dwarfs worked hard over their forges behind doors of stone. These bent and twisted creatures never saw the light of sun nor the green meadow grass.

When Loki asked Ivaldi's sons to make hair of pure gold, proudly they said, "Golden hair is perhaps the least of what Ivaldi's sons can make for the Gods."

"Show me," Loki said.

The dwarfs went to work. The forge was hot, and the sound of their hammers rang throughout the caves. When they were finished, Loki had three gifts for the Gods: for Sif, pure gold hair that would start to grow the minute it touched her head; a magic spear called Gungnir, which would always find its mark; and the best ship of all, called Skidbladnir, which could carry all the Gods and their weapons, create its own fair breeze the moment the sails were raised, and be folded to fit into a man's pocket.

"Very good," Loki said. "Bring these gifts to the court of the Gods for Odin to judge. I will meet you there tomorrow."

Loki then went to the cave of a dwarf named Brokkr, who was the ugliest of all the dwarfs in Nidavellir, and possibly the meanest, but whose brother Sindri was the finest smith. Loki told him what the sons of Ivaldi had made for the Gods.

"I will wager my head that you cannot make three gifts that are greater," Loki said boldly.

Brokkr frowned, and when he did, his wiry brows furled so they covered his eyes. "All right," the dwarf said, "but you stay away. No one comes near when Sindri puts his irons in the fire."

Brokkr took up the bellows, and Sindri put a piece of pig's hide into the fire. "Keep blowing, brother," he warned Brokkr, "or all will be ruined." The brothers worked hard. Loki, hoping to get the gifts without having to forfeit his head, sent a fly to bother Brokkr as he pumped the bellows. Just as Sindri reached into the furnace, the fly bit Brokkr's hand, but the dwarf did not stop pumping. Sindri drew a beautiful boar from the forge, with bristles and mane of pure gold. "Good," he said, and named the boar Fearful-Tusk.

Once again Sindri put his tongs and metals in the fire, and once more Loki's fly bit Brokkr, but the dwarf did not stop pumping. Sindri drew a golden ring out of the fire, which he called Draupnir. Every ninth night eight gold rings of equal value dropped from it.

The third time Sindri put a huge piece of iron in the fire, he especially warned Brokkr not to let up on the bellows, as the slightest cooling would ruin his work. Loki's fly bit Brokkr on his eyelid, causing blood to run into his eye. Brokkr took one hand off the bellows to wipe his eye, and Sindri yelled, "Blow, brother, blow!"

Sindri drew a huge hammer out of the fire, which he named Mjollnir. It had the power to crush anything it fell upon, to fly straight at any target, and always to return to the hand of the owner. The only flaw in the hammer was that its handle was too short, caused by the cooling of the fire when Brokkr wiped his eye.

"Fine work," Loki told Brokkr and Sindri. "Bring the gifts to Odin's court, and he will judge us both."

When the court opened the next morning, the Gods were still angry at Loki. Sif sat on a bench at the side, the scarf over her head ample testimony to his crime. Loki did not look at her, but went straight to where Odin, Freyr, and Thor sat in judgment.

Loki brought out the magic spear Ivaldi's sons had made and gave it to Odin. "With this fine weapon you can fight any giant who threatens you," he said.

Then Loki reached into his pocket and took out the magic ship, Skidbladnir, and put it into Freyr's hands. Freyr was not impressed—for it was very small—but his eyes widened when Loki told him how fast the ship would go when its sails were unfurled.

"Very well," Freyr said. "I will believe that when I see it. But still our lovely Sif has no hair."

Loki then brought out the strands of pure gold that Ivaldi's sons had made, and took them to Sif. He lifted her scarf, and the moment he touched the gold to her head, it took root and flowed luxuriously glistening down her back. Sif smiled happily at Thor and turned to let everyone see.

"Now have I atoned for my crime, and will you let me go free?" Loki asked.

"How do we know you will not commit other crimes?" the Highest God asked.

"Just this," Loki replied, and called to Brokkr to enter the court. "Tell Odin of our bargain," he said to the dwarf.

Brokkr said, "The sly one has promised me his

head if my brother Sindri's forgings are greater than those of Ivaldi's sons."

Odin nodded and said, "Show us what Sindri has wrought, and we will judge."

Brokkr gave Freyr the boar with the golden mane and told him that it could carry him over water and through air; the animal was loyal and as fast as any horse; the glow from its mane would light the way through the darkness of night, or any fog or gloom.

Then Brokkr put into Thor's hand the great hammer, Mjollnir, and into Odin's hand Brokkr put the treasured ring, Draupnir.

The three Gods talked together and weighed the worth of the gifts. Each prized his own treasure, but finally they decided that the hammer, in Thor's strong hand, would be most valuable of all.

Odin said to Loki, "You have done well with the dwarfs; these are such fine gifts that we would gladly let you stay in Asgard. But since Mjollnir is the greatest, you must be true to your word and give Brokkr your head."

"Not fair!" Loki cried.

"A God must keep his word," Odin said.

Loki turned to Brokkr. "Won't you let me off? Is it not enough to know you have won?"

"Certainly not," Brokkr said. "A promise is a promise. Your head is the treasure I covet."

"Take it then if you can," Loki snapped at him and flew off on his magic shoes right over the heads of everyone in court. Just at the door Thor caught and held him by the ankle, dragged him back to Brokkr, and held him down so Brokkr could take his head. Brokkr ran his finger along the blade of his long knife, eyeing Loki's neck carefully.

Loki, trying to squirm out of Thor's strong hands,

made a last, desperate try. "I promised you my head but not my neck," he cried. "You may have no part of my neck, not even a hair!"

It worked. Brokkr growled in frustrated anger, and put down the knife. "Liar," the old dward grumbled. "Cheat! I'll never trust the word of a God again!" He sewed Loki's lying lips together, but Loki opened his mouth and broke the thongs. Ever after he could feel the scars where Brokkr's needle had pierced his lips.

While Hugin and Munin searched the world over for signs of the clever god, Loki had actually returned to Asgard. Odin was too late. No one noticed that Loki was there because all the Gods were so engrossed in their delightful sport of throwing weapons at Balder and testing Frigga's promises. Loki stood watching in the shadows. At first he was astounded by the startling sight of spear after spear falling to the ground—stopped, it appeared, in midair by some unseen force.

Then his astonishment turned to jealousy. Why should Balder be so wonderfully protected against harm? Loki could feel each twinge of pain he had endured when off hunting giants with Thor. He thought of his bruises at the hands of Thjazi, and he remembered the pain of hunger in Skrymir's land. What had Balder ever done to gain such love and such good fortune? Who was he to have such attention? Had Balder given the Gods such gifts as Draupnir, Mjollnir, or Skidbladnir?

He ran his finger over his scarred lips, determined to find out what magic Frigga had used to protect her favorite son. If magic were possible—well, wasn't he a master magician too?

Late that afternoon, when the evening shadows were long and the Gods and heroes were quietly waiting for the time of the evening feast, Loki disguised himself as one of Frigga's servants and went to Fensalir.

He found Frigga alone, and he could not help remembering how often she had turned against him. Not even when he had tried to help Thor win against Utgard-Loki's wiles had Frigga trusted him or believed he was loyal.

He said in his most ingratiating voice, "Isn't it wonderful to see that nothing can harm Balder?"

Frigga smiled and said yes, and asked her servant to bring her shawl, as it was nearly time for the feast.

"I've been away," Loki said. "When I left, everyone thought Balder would die. Now I find he is not afraid of anyone or anything."

"No," Frigga said, "nothing can harm Balder now." She spoke proudly. "I have seen to that."

"You must be very clever," Loki said softly. "How can you be sure?"

"Neither weapon nor element nor man nor beast can harm my son," she said. "I have taken an oath from them all."

Loki pulled his woman's cloak around him more closely. "Have you not forgotten any?"

"No," Frigga said, "I have been thorough." She closed her feathered shawl and stood up. "Only one little plant did not swear," she said, as if just remembering. "In the woods west of Valhalla there was a little green shrub which seemed too young and weak to swear an oath. It is called the mistletoe. . . ."

The branch which seemed
so slender and fair
Full grown in strength the
mistletoe stood,
A harmful shaft that Hoder
hurled.

Loki left Frigga as quickly as he could and ran to the western woods, following the same course he had travelled long ago when he had lured Idun to the giant Thjazi. The woods were different now. Wind whipped through the trees, tearing the crisp leaves from their branches, pulling at Loki's clothing. It was the time of the year, he knew, when in Midgard the sun circled so low that many of the valleys were dark and men milked their cows by seal-oil lamp.

Loki searched frantically. To find one twig in a whole forest would be impossible, he thought unhappily. He looked up to the treetops, turned himself around three times. No science would help him now—it was growing so dark. He must trust to luck, or magic. On the wind he heard laughter, and remembering the gaiety of the Gods playing with Balder, he felt an old anger choke him. No one ever had laughed with *him* that way. He was always alone, it seemed, unacceptable to the Gods and unacceptable to the giants. No one wanted him. It wasn't fair!

Alone and miserable, he suddenly wondered what he was doing by himself in this dark forest on such an impossible search! Why did he not just forget those unguarded words of Frigga's! Let Balder live! He tasted the idea for a moment and found it not unpleasant. He might even join the others, take a turn at their game! He began to feel better when he came to a clearing in the woods where the moss was soft under his feet and the wind did not blow. In the middle was a great green oak tree with spreading branches and a gnarled trunk so wide that two men could not have held hands around it. A little green shoot grew from the stump of an old broken branch. Loki held his breath and touched the thick little leaf hesitantly, noting the tight clusters of waxy white berries. He knew well what it was, and for an agonizing moment he wondered why he had been unlucky enough to find it!

Unhappily he knew that he would have to pluck it, that—given the opportunity—he would not be able to help himself. He argued with himself. He could take the mistletoe, but he did not have to *use* it. He could give the Gods one last chance to welcome him, to accept him as one of them at last. If they did, he would burn the lethal branch, and Balder would be safe forever. Then Loki would be even more heroic than Frigga!

Loki snapped off the sprig of mistletoe and flew back to Asgard. The feast was going strong, both light and laughter pouring out of Valhalla's many doors. Loki smiled wryly. The Gods might not laugh so loudly, he thought, if they knew what power he held in his hand.

Loki stepped into the great stone hall, and at first no one noticed his presence. He looked down the long row of seats to where the Gods were. There was a visitor in the hall this night, and Bragi was weaving his stories of the history of the Gods. He was telling of the great contest between Thor and the giants, and he told of the kidnaping of Idun and of Loki's wager with the dwarf Brokkr, and how Loki had nearly lost his head. Bragi was speaking well, and the visitor was impressed. Loki stepped into the light and walked along the table, and as he approached, Bragi began the story of Balder's dreams and how Frigga had thwarted the fates. Suddenly Odin saw Loki and held up his hand for Bragi to stop.

"What are you doing in Asgard?" Odin asked Loki cautiously.

"I am thirsty," Loki replied. "I have journeyed a long way today. Is there not some mead for me and a seat in this hall of heroes?"

The Gods did not answer. They never did enjoy having Loki join their feasting—this night above all. Finally Bragi said coolly, "Well, tonight I'm afraid there is no place for you, for our noble visitor is in the last seat."

Loki burned with anger and turned to Odin, speaking through tense lips. "Remember, Odin," he said bitterly, "in days of old our blood did mix! *Then* you promised to pour no wine unless it were poured for us both!" He turned, and before Odin could speak or offer him mead, Loki stalked out of the hall. He crept away for the remainder of the night and slept at the edge of the woods, his hand tightly clenched around the mistletoe branch.

In the morning some of the Gods gathered in the courtyard with the heroes and played their usual game. The sound of sticks and stones and clanging spears echoed off the cobbled court. Balder the innocent, pure and happy, stood smiling at the crowd while their missiles flew harmlessly toward him.

Loki watched unseen from a shadowed doorway. Suddenly he noticed Hoder standing near him, outside the circle of laughing Gods and heroes, quiet and alone with his own dark thoughts.

Loki moved close to Hoder and spoke in his ear. "Wouldn't you like to join in the fun?" he asked.

Hoder shook his head. "I cannot see to aim," he said. "And besides, I have no weapon."

"Take this." Loki, his heart pounding, put the mistletoe into Hoder's hand and carefully held his arm. He thought, Revenge at last! as he guided Hoder's willing hand, starting the motion toward Balder.

Not knowing the power of what he held, nor meaning any harm, Hoder threw the tiny sliver. It flew quick and true and pierced the heart of Balder.

Balder fell to the stone floor, and then the yard was silent. No one laughed. No sound echoed off the walls. Loki held his breath, for suddenly he realized the terrible chain of events he had set in motion. There was a bitter taste in his mouth, and tight bands of fear seemed to bind his chest. He knew well what for a moment he had forgotten—there were no rewards, no leaping joys, for avengers or for haters.

Hoder cocked his head as he always did toward the sounds of motion, but now there was no motion, no stirring of air, no sound.

Tyr stood like a silent statue, a stone in his hand, ready to let fly. Thor, who had bent over to pick up a spear, was still half bent, frozen, it seemed, by the sight of Balder lying so still on the cobbles, the little green sliver protruding from his chest.

If the Gods who were in the court at that moment breathed, even their breathing made no sound, as if when Balder dropped they had been turned to stone.

Hoder brushed the air in front of his eyes, as if to clear a mist, and he said quietly, "What is it?"

No one answered.

Bragi wet his lips and went to where Balder lay. He took the mistletoe in his hand and gently pulled it from Balder's chest, and then he put his head down and listened. There was no heartbeat, no breath.

Hoder said louder, "What is it? Why is everyone so quiet?"

No one answered. No one moved. Then Bragi held up the branch and looked around the circle of Gods until his eyes came to Hoder. He shook his head, and tears silently flowed from his gentle blue eyes.

"Someone is crying," Hoder said. "What is it? What has happened to Balder?"

The silent Vidar, one of Odin's most valiant sons, stood with his sword half raised and opened his mouth to answer, but no words came. Balder could not be dead! Vidar could not believe what he saw. Frigga had been promised. Everything had promised Frigga not to harm Balder!

Freyr put his hand over his eyes, as if to shield the sight of the shining god dead before him. Which was the dream? Which was the truth? None of them knew. None of them could tell Hoder what he already knew from the sound of the silence of death around him.

Finally Bragi took the mistletoe and put it in Hoder's hand. "Is this what you threw at Balder?"

Hoder closed his fingers around the twig, feeling once again its young slenderness, and nodded. "What is it?" he asked.

"Only a little mistletoe," Bragi said, "but it flew so straight and true that some marksman of rare genius must have guided its course. What angry soul put this weapon into your blind hand?"

"I don't know."

Bragi said nothing, but all the Gods looked at him and shook their heads.

Finally Hoder spoke again, his voice so pinched and tight that everyone knew he did not want to hear the answer. "Tell me, Bragi, what have I done?"

"Balder is dead," the poet said gently. "Balder is dead."

Like a chorus the Gods said, "Balder is dead. Balder is dead."

Hoder stood still, his arms hung at his sides, and tears silently ran down his craggy cheeks.

"Balder is dead, Balder is dead," the Gods began to chant and weep. One by one, others joined the mournful dirge until the sound, "Balder is dead, Balder is dead," could be heard all over Asgard and the worlds below.

Loki, who had been watching, slipped around the corner of the courtyard wall, but Freyr caught a glimpse of him.

"There he goes!" the bright god cried. "After him!"

"After him!" Thor echoed, and the two gods rushed away.

The heroes wept and cried and stormed, blaming first one and then another. Why had they toyed with

Balder's death? they asked. And they cursed themselves for fools.

Then even wise old Njord, who never cursed or raged with passions of anger, raised his arms to the sky and uttered an oath and swore revenge. The dirge went on. "Balder is dead, Balder is dead." And many who had not been in the courtyard came at the mournful sound.

Suddenly Odin appeared and raised his arms. "Stop! Silence!" he commanded.

"Balder is dead, Balder is dead," the chorus went on and on.

"Enough of your wailing," Odin's booming voice rang out. "Remember where you are! There shall be no violence or vengeance in this hallowed hall."

The crowd became quiet. The Father-of-All walked to where Balder lay and knelt down by his most beautiful son. Gently he crossed Balder's arms over his chest, and into the right hand Odin put his own treasured ring, Draupnir, and closed the dead fingers around it. Then the One-Eyed One stood up and faced the silent circle of his children.

His voice was heavy. "So Balder is dead. The Vala spoke truth." Odin looked at Hoder, still holding the mistletoe in his hand. "Son in darkness, your hand was only a slave to a rune written long ago. There will be an end to your pain." Then Odin turned to the others. "The time has come for us to prepare Balder's ship, which will be his funeral pyre. The balefire we build for Balder will burn as brightly as his soul was pure. There shall be no ash to stain the memory of his perfect spirit. And in each child of man his unstained soul shall be reborn." Odin paused. "To work!" he cried out. "You know well what must be done!"

The Gods and heroes turned to leave, but suddenly Frigga swept into the yard, her feathers ruffled and her eyes dark.

"Wait!" she called to the Gods. "Do not leave yet! We have not done all we could!"

The Gods stopped and looked at Odin, whose orders they were following. "Are we going to accept Balder's death like helpless children? Without my son we all will die!" Frigga cried.

"But what can we do now?" Hoenir asked. "Balder is already in Hel's hands. We are helpless!"

"Is there not one of you brave enough to go after him?"

The Gods looked at each other and then at Odin.

"Impossible," Odin said. "The fates knew long ago this would happen. No one comes back from Hel's domain."

"But I have defied fate once and won," Frigga persisted.

"Odin is right," Vidar said. "We believed you before and now Balder is dead. Why did you not take an oath from the mistletoe?"

Frigga lifted her chin proudly. "I took no account of it," she said, "because of its youth. That was my mistake." She shook the tears from her eyes. "But who among you is brave enough to follow Balder to Niflheim, land of the dead, and bargain with Hel for his return? Balder does not belong with her! Only cowards, the sick and the aged, the evil in mind and the callous in spirit belong to Hel. Is there not one god among all of you who would risk his life to bring Balder back to Asgard?"

The Gods and heroes knew that no live person had ever crossed the bridge to Hel and entered the high gates; and no dead man or hero or God had ever returned.

Hoder spoke softly. "Let me go," he said. "I threw the mistletoe. Let me be the one to bring my brother back. I am useless here. If Hel will keep me instead of Balder, my own life will at least have had some purpose."

"No, Hoder," Odin said. "You may not go. The road is long, and the turns are too many. Only a swift and sure-footed, well-sighted messenger has any chance of finding the way."

Hermod, the nimble god, rose and said that he was not afraid to go. "I will gladly give my life," he said. "You must not lose your best fighters, like Thor or Freyr, or silent Vidar, whose huge foot has such strength. You will need their help in Asgard if the giants invade. But I can travel fast and far, and I have sometimes bargained wisely."

Frigga nodded and said, "You have often carried messages well for Odin and for me." She took a hawk feather from her shawl and gave it to Hermod. "This will help speed you on your way," she said.

Odin spoke. "It is a long and dangerous trip to the land of the dead. You must travel through each of the nine worlds, through lands of our friends and our enemies. You must get past the maiden guard of the Gjoll bridge, which spans the roaring river before Hel's gate. You will meet the bloody hound, who will try to frighten you away. You will ride across the graves of many men, and you must not be afraid. In the middle of Niflheim itself you must not fall into the well, Hvergelmir, which is guarded by the serpent Nidhogg, who lies on the corpse-covered bank and chews at the roots of our tree of life, sapping its strength."

"I will not be afraid," Hermod said. "I will go."

"Good," said Frigga. She sank to her knees beside Balder.

"Take my horse, Sleipnir," Odin said. "There is no faster animal in Asgard. Sleipnir knows the way."

Odin was the first to leave the courtyard. He walked with the long-haired goddess Rind, whose singing was clearer and more melancholy than any bird, whose lyric voice told stories of love as beautifully as Bragi's poetry related heroic deeds. Odin took Rind's arm, and together they walked past Valhalla, over the hill to the Western Hall, which was her home.

Hoder stood in the doorway and listened to his mother weep over the body of her dead son.

Hermod saddled Sleipnir and rode toward the rainbow.

*Bale and hatred I bring to
the Gods,
And their mead with venom
I mix.*

—L

When Loki flew on his
magic shoes out of the
courtyard, the sound of
the dirge followed him far.
He, too, wept as he flew, for a part of him wished
that he had not done what he did, that his actions
could have been for love, not hate, for honor and
glory, not destruction and desolation. It seemed that
when others sinned or committed small crimes, their
punishments were slight. But when he spoke, his
words turned to swords; and when he did the Gods
mischief, all the world suffered. It had always been
that way.

He knew that each of the Gods had a part to play
in the grand design of life and death that was written
when Odin made the world. His own role of doer of
mischief that led to evil was his own tragedy. He
had a many-faceted part to play, for there was, he
knew, a little bit of him in every man and God, and

it was *that* that each must fight, and so fight him!

He flew as fast and as far as he could for he knew the Gods would follow him. The hiding place he found was behind the highest waterfall—called Franang's Falls—in the farthest corner of the world. There he found a house with four windows, from which he could watch in all directions. By day he became a salmon that swam in the river below the falls, and by night he sat in the house and wove a net. There he stayed, alone as ever.

One night he heard thunder over the hills. He looked to the west and saw a streak of light cross the sky. He knew the thunder was Thor approaching, and the light was the mane of Freyr's boar. By morning they would find him. He put the fishnet he had woven with such care into the fire and, turning himself into a salmon again, dove into the river. When Thor and Freyr arrived at the house, it was empty but for a little heap of ashes in the corner. They looked out of all the windows and searched the horizons for the villain's route, but they saw nothing. Then Freyr noticed a little piece of netting in the ashes and showed it to Thor.

"That magician has become a fish," Thor exclaimed. "He can be anything. Now I know where to find him!" They walked out and looked at Franang's Falls, crashing from the cliffside, foaming into the riverbottom. Thor saw a glint of pink and silver under the water and cried, "There he is!" and strode into the river. Just as he reached the fish, the salmon jumped out of the water and swam upstream away from him. No matter how Thor tried, no matter how quick he was, he could not catch the salmon. "At least we have him trapped," Thor said to Freyr.

"He will not swim from here to the icy ocean where the serpent may still lie in wait, and he cannot jump these falls. Go to Asgard and ask Odin for help."

Freyr climbed onto his swift, bright-maned boar and flew to Asgard. He brought back with him a dozen of the Gods and heroes to help catch Loki. The Gods made a new net, wide enough to reach all the way across the river, and Thor tried to chase the salmon into it. Three times they thought they had him, and three times the slippery fish got away. Finally Thor realized that Loki could hide between stones at the bottom of the river, so they weighted the net and stretched it across the river again, half the Gods on one side of the river and half on the other. Thor strode up the center of the raging stream. To escape him now, the salmon either had to leap the falls or leap over Thor's head and wide reach. First the frantic fish tried to jump the falls, but they were too high, and he fell back into the rushes. Thor and the Gods closed in on him. Finally, when they were very close, the salmon jumped high into the air past Thor's head, and would have cleared the net if the great God had not grabbed the tail as it went by him. Slippery as it was, Thor held tight, keeping the fish out of water and squeezing so hard he tapered the shape of the salmon's tail forever. Finally Loki changed back into his own form and, gasping for breath, begged for mercy.

Thor held him down on his back. The Gods looked at him pitilessly. Oh, he was helpless enough, they thought, now that he had done his mischief! They considered how to punish him. Thor would have killed him right there, but Freyr and Tyr and the wise Forseti protested.

"We should not let him die so easily," Tyr said. "When the sun falls out of the sky, Loki should see it!"

"His suffering should be prolonged," Freyr said. "For his destruction of Balder the whole world will suffer."

With the gut of a wolf for rope, the Gods tied Loki on his back to three tall flagstones, so that he might never rest and never escape. However he twisted and turned, the stones cut into his flesh. The Gods placed him on a ledge on the side of a cliff, where the sound of the pounding surf could reach his ears. Over his head they trapped a serpent, whose burning venom dripped onto his face.

Over and over he begged the Gods to let him go. He offered them new treasures and made rash promises, but the Gods were unrelenting.

Freyr tightened the last knot and said, "Always before this we have forgiven you, and we have taken you back among us in Asgard. But each time you returned to betray us. You have turned love into hate, beauty into ugliness, order into chaos, a compassionate brother into a murderer. No, here you shall stay forever until the world comes to an end." As Freyr spoke, the entrails of the wolf turned to iron.

"What about you, Forseti?" Loki begged, tears in his eyes. Forseti had reconciled many arguments, and was always fair in his judgments. "Will you at least remember some of the good I have done for the Gods? Will you set me free?"

Forseti looked at Loki on his bed of stone. "No," Balder's son said, "I will not let you go free. You have robbed my innocent father of life, my blind uncle of conscience. But I will pity you so long as

you remain bound. My judgment is to allow Sigyn to sit by your side, where a good wife belongs. She may hold a cup to catch the serpent's venom so it need not drip on your face. Here you both shall stay until the final battle, Ragnarok, the end of the world."

Then the Gods left Loki's wife Sigyn beside him catching the venom as it dripped. But when her cup became full, she turned to empty it, and a few burning drops fell onto Loki's cheek. Then he cried out and twisted against his irons in such agony that the whole world shook.

In Asgard the preparations for the great funeral were proceeding. Thor and Freyr told Odin of Loki's punishment. "Now is Balder's death revenged?" Thor asked the Wise One.

Odin did not answer. He knew it was not Loki's hand that had killed Balder, and he knew the ways of the fates had been made clear to him by the dead wise woman long ago. He looked to the horizon, where the sun still hung, and he thought of Hermod, travelling the long road to Niflheim. He looked to the hill where Breidablik stood, and where now Balder's servants gathered his belongings. He thought of the sights he had seen in Mimir's murky well that misty night long ago.

Odin said, "Loki is my brother, and we are like two sides of a coin. When you punish him, you punish me. His pain will end when mine begins. I have created a world and all brothers in it, and that is what I must remember, and what I had to face in Mimir's well."

"What did you see in Mimir's well?" Freyr asked the Great Magician.

"Reflections," Odin said, "and the night was dark, and only Asgard lay in the heavy clouds over my

16: NJORD'S LONELINESS

*To me the wailing of wolves
seemed ill
After the song of swans*
    —*Njord*

Hermod's ride to the land of the dead took nine days and nine nights, and he learned much on the way.

On the first day the sun rose high and shone long enough for him to pass every dwelling in Asgard from Skadi's mountaintop to Njord's home, Noatun—Ship's Haven—by the sea. Everyone stopped him and offered him good wishes and advice to guide him on his long, dangerous journey from Yggdrasil's leafy top to the river in Hel's land beneath its deepest root.

It was late afternoon when he reached Njord's seaside home. The old god came out of his tall-timbered temple and held up his hand for Hermod to stop. The sky was as gray as the sea behind him, and the clouds as turbulent as the water. Njord's long gray beard lay like another fold on the dark blue cloak that fell from his shoulders to his feet, and his soft gray eyes and the deep lines on his cheeks spoke of the patience of long, lonely years.

"So you ride on Sleipnir to bargain with Hel," said the god of the sea. "What makes Odin think he can trust the old hag to let you return?"

"I have no fear of the hag," Hermod said. "Frigga's will is as strong as Odin's wisdom. I am the messenger of the highest goddess and the Wisest-of-All, and their rightfulness will protect me."

"Odin was not always wise," Njord said softly, "and Hel knows as much."

"What do you mean, old man?" Hermod said indignantly. "If you were truly of the race of the Gods you would not speak so irreverently of the All-Father!"

Njord nodded his head and closed his eyes a moment, as if searching for memories or the right words to speak. "Yes," he said, "I was born to the race of the Wanes, and I was their chief. They are good people and have always been so. And since the war with the Gods they have been friends. The Wanes won that war, you know." He paused, and Hermod tried not to look surprised. "Did you ever wonder why Balder must die?" Njord asked suddenly.

Hermod frowned. "What are you getting at?" he asked.

"You will find a new kind of truth on your way through the nine worlds," Njord said. "As you travel through the land of my past, remember that I am the victim of Odin's first sin. Find out who threw the first spear and thus brought war to the world! To some it might seem that Loki—Odin's blood brother—is not the only God whose hand guided the mistletoe!"

"You have lost your mind," Hermod said. "You

are talking in riddles. The crying of the seafowl by your watery home has muddled your brain."

"It might seem so at first," Njord replied, "but the sea birds are my friends. And so is every man and every God who travels over or through the water. Few stay to visit with me here, so I am nearly always alone."

"You are alone too much," Hermod said.

"But I know more than you think," the old man said. "We cannot all live forever in the land of our birth." His words were wistful but Hermod did not believe now that Njord was without reason. "It was written long ago that I should live my life in loneliness, with only my seals and wild birds for company."

Hermod felt sorry that he had spoken harshly, for he knew that Njord was the finest of Gods, who governed the course of the wind, calmed the angry sea after a storm, and tempered fire. Men on earth always looked to Njord for good harvests, safe voyages, and consistent weather. Njord's son and daughter, Freyr and Freyja, were brilliant and energetic, and Asgard would have been poorer indeed without them.

But Njord's marriage to Skadi, the daughter of the giant Thjazi, had been brief and unhappy. After the Gods had killed her father and Odin had cast Thjazi's eyes up to the sky, Skadi had come weeping and wailing to the gates of Asgard. Odin was compassionate, and told Skadi that to make up for the loss of her father she could choose any God for her husband, so long as she made the selection by seeing only his feet. Skadi stopped her crying and agreed that if she had one of the Gods as her husband, life on the mountaintop, Thrymheim, would not be so lonely.

Odin had called the Gods together and lined them up behind a screen. Skadi carefully inspected the feet of each one and stopped at the ones that were most clean and straight and beautifully shaped. They must be the feet of Balder, she thought, for it would be true that the most beautiful God should have the most beautiful feet. But when the screen was removed, she found that she had picked Njord for her husband.

"How can I marry him?" Skadi asked unhappily. "I cannot live with the water as my home. You promised me a God to come to Thrymheim!"

"How can I rule the tides and the seafolk," Njord asked, "if I am remote on some high mountain? No, if you want to be my bride you just come to live in my Ship's Haven, the tall-timbered Noatun."

Skadi wept and Njord stood firm. Finally Odin suggested a compromise; first they would live nine nights on Skadi's mountain in Thrymheim together, and then they would live nine nights in Noatun, by the sea. So should their marriage be.

Skadi and Njord agreed, and the marriage took place. Njord followed Skadi up to Thrymheim, where Thjazi had lived, and there he stayed the full nine nights. When he came down the mountain, he had tears in his eyes, and he sang:

"Loath were the hills to me. I was not long in them—
Nights only nine. The wailing of the wolves
    seemed ill
After the song of swans. I will not return."

And so Skadi, who had learned to love this gentle god, followed her husband down to his seaside home, and there they spent three days and three nights.

fter that short time she came weeping to Odin's
ourt, singing a mournful song.

"You have your god-husband," Odin said. "Now
hat more do you want?"

Skadi sang as tears rolled down her cheeks:

"Sleep could I never on the sea-beds,
    For the wailing of the waterfowl.
    He wakens me who comes from the deep!"

Skadi returned to Thrymheim and never stayed
vith Njord again. She lived alone on her snow-covered
nountaintop and travelled about on snowshoes hunt-
ng wild beasts with her bow and arrow. Men came
o call her the Snow Goddess. Njord stayed by the
vater he loved and seldom came away from his home.

Hermod listened to the breaking waves and the
ry of a gull from the roof of Noatun. He knew that
Vjord would not speak lightly or untruthfully to him.
Tell me what I will learn in the land of your past,"
le said finally to the wise old god. But Njord did
.ot seem to hear him.

"Listen before you speak. Do not fight before you
hink. No one wants to die in a strange land." Then
Vjord waved Hermod on his way and called after
dim, "When you cross the seas, they will stay calm.
have hope."

Hermod finally reached Bifrost as the sun sank
)elow the mountain. He said his last goodby to Heim-
lall on the rainbow bridge. A cool, damp wind
ouched his cheeks as Sleipnir carried him through
he evening mists over the forests toward the seas of
Vanaheim, land of the Wanes.

*On the host his spear did
Odin hurl;
Then in the world did the
war come.*

The sun did not rise quite so high on the second morning, and Hermod urged Sleipnir to hurry. He knew he must pass all the way through this country that had more water than land before darkness came again. The Wanes stood on the shores of the many lakes and rivers, bays and deep-cut sounds, watching Sleipnir gallop by. Hermod did not stop to talk with them, but he waited for some sign of the truths that Njord said he would find along the way. He thought of the old god's warning, and he wondered what he had meant. Odin had never spoken of the war with the Wanes, and Hermod had not known that the Wanes had won. No one, in fact, had ever told him what the war was about, and as long as he could remember, the Wanes had been friendly.

Just as the eight-legged horse and its rider came to the edge of the ocean and the sun touched the rim of the world, three women climbed out of the waves nd stood dripping before him. They were all the ame height and of the same slender, long-legged grace, and though their finely drawn features were like as triplets, one was old and hollow-eyed, and one had the full, mellowed firmness of middle years, and one's lips and smooth cheeks were as ripe and fresh and full as a barely grown girl. Their skin was pale, and the cloth that they wore draped about their slender bodies was the color of mist or the ocean's spray.

Hermod reined Sleipnir to a stop.

"Where are you going?" the first woman asked.

"I am going to Niflheim to bargain with Hel for Balder's return," Hermod replied courteously.

"Who killed Balder?" the second woman asked. "I thought all of us had promised to protect him."

"His blind brother threw the lethal weapon," the third woman said. "It was already written."

"If Balder is dead, then the end is near for the Gods," the young woman said. "Beware of Ragnarok."

"You'll not get Balder back. You'll not find the way! Only Odin, the One-Eyed One knows the road to Niflheim and back," the old woman said. "I have seen him go and come."

"Who are you to be telling me these things?" Hermod asked.

"We are the three wise maidens of Vanaheim," the middle one said, "Past, Present, and Future."

"Stand aside and let me go," Hermod said firmly. "I am Odin's messenger, and I will follow his orders only."

"Odin knows well how men must listen to us," Future said. "So it was agreed after the war he started."

"What do you mean?"

Past answered him with the following story. As the old woman spoke the waves crested and broke around her feet, like a musical accompaniment to her words.

In the morning of time, when the Gods were innocent and lived in peace and the land of men was barely born, three Wane maidens went down to Midgard. They spoke with the first men there and gave them rules to live by. They told men their destinies.

Odin heard of this and became angry. He ordered the maidens to come before him. "Who are you to set the fates of men?" he asked. "I made the world and all things in it. The Gods rule the cosmos! I brought order out of chaos," he added proudly. "Men must worship us and look to us for truth and knowledge. How dare you write the future as if you had the power of Gods!"

The Wane maidens paid no attention to Odin's warning. They polished pieces of wood and carved laws into them, and said these runes would control the happenings in the world of men.

Now all the Gods were as angry as Odin. They went to Vanaheim and captured a Wane woman whose name was Gollveig—Mighty Gold. They told the maidens to destroy the runes or Gollveig would burn.

The three maidens refused. The Gods built a fire in a stone chamber of Valhalla, and there they burned the woman. As the flames consumed her, a figure of pure gold appeared and rose right out of the fire. The Gods fell back in astonishment.

"Burn the Wane woman again!" Odin ordered his servants.

Again the Gods built a fire around Gollveig, and

again she rose out of the flames, pure gold. A third time they tried, and a third time the golden female rose. Now the Gods were frightened.

"Are the Wanes so great?" Tyr asked Odin, "that they can turn ashes to gold?"

"Is this a sign from a power greater than yours?" Frigga asked. "Let Gollveig go! She has not harmed us. Perhaps it *is* right for them to tell the future!"

Suddenly there was a tremendous clamoring outside the gates of Asgard. The Gods rushed to the wall and looked outside. Hundreds of Wanes were pressing and pounding at the gates, chanting and calling for Gollveig's return. Odin called his best warriors and his strongest heroes around him. Although the Gods were outnumbered, Odin stood firm.

"Gollveig must burn," he roared, "unless you revere the Gods who have created order among men!"

The Wanes massed together and, shoulder to shoulder, tried to storm the gates of heaven itself. Odin was so angry when he saw this that he took his spear and hurled it into the gathering force. The first war began.

The battle between God and Wane raged, and spears clashed, and suddenly the gates and the great high walls of Asgard broke. The invading Wanes rushed into the breach and spread over all of Asgard. The Gods were defeated, but the Wanes took no prisoners.

The highest of the Wanes called the highest of the Gods together, and they met in council. After many days they wrote a treaty. To insure permanent peace and respect for the agreement, they exchanged hostages. Men should be able to worship either God or Wane, they agreed, or even both at once. The Gods had to admit that the Wanes were their equals, that peace would come from the sharing of their realms and their wisdom. Njord, the chief of the Wanes, went to live in Asgard, and he brought to the Gods the knowledge of the sea people. Hoenir went to live in Vanaheim, but he was so timid the Wanes soon tired of him, and he returned to Asgard and lived among the Gods.

"So you see," Past told Hermod, "it was Odin's spear that began the first war, and he alone has known what was written in the runes."

Present said, "But since then the Wanes and the Gods have lived in peace, and we know, as Hermod does, that Balder in life was a joy but his death threatens us all. Let us send Hermod on with our blessings and our hope."

Future said, "One who dares ride to Niflheim and bargain with Hel is brave indeed. The Gods have paid high costs for their mistakes. I will write no more runes. Go, Hermod, brave messenger of the All-Father. Do not open your eyes too widely in Alfheim if you want to see your way. Ride in safety!"

Before Hermod could answer, the three maidens turned and sank into the waves. Then he heard only the chorus of the water as he urged Sleipnir to travel once more. They rode into the darkening sky.

18: THE LAST FRIENDLY WORLD

And Alfheim the Gods to
Freyr once gave
As a toothgift in ancient time

The dawn of the third day came, but the sun's rays did not warm Sleipnir's rump nor Hermod's back, for the mists that hung over Alfheim were so thick that only the closest rise and fall in the land was visible ahead. Yet Hermod spurred Sleipnir to a gallop, and the stones rolled clattering beneath his eight hooves. There were miles and miles of copses, hillocks, rock-strewn hillsides to cross before the day was done.

No sooner had Hermod wished for the shining mane of Freyr's wonderful boar, Fearful-Tusk, to light his way through the gloom than the fog lifted just enough to reveal hundreds of tiny, glittering little elves, darting and winking like jewels in the rocks, peeking out at Hermod, dodging away from Sleipnir's hooves. Hermod knew none of the elves by name, but he did not fear them, for he knew they would not purposely harm him. The reason they ran and hid, he knew, was that if one of the elves were to come squarely before his eyes, the brightness might burn and blind him, just as the magnification of a sun's ray focused on a single point can set a dry leaf on fire. Hermod smiled at the enchanted sight that surrounded him, for the creatures coming and going in the light-diffusing mist looked like the phosphorescence of the sea. How appropriate, he thought, that Odin should have given this land of bright elves as a toothgift to Freyr for his special keeping. From the beginning of his life Freyr had loved the brilliance of the sun and every bright and shining thing that approached its power.

Long ago, when Freyr first came to Asgard, he had looked into Jotunheim just as the beautiful giantess, Gerd, left her father's house. Gerd raised her right arm, which was brilliant enough to light all the land and sky. Freyr was so dazzled that he became sick with love and longing for Gerd.

He said to his servant Skirnir, "Go down to Jotunheim and bring that woman back for me. Because I am a God, I cannot beg favors of anyone of the giant race. Yet I will neither eat nor drink until Gerd becomes my wife."

Gerd's father was a powerful giant and surrounded his home with a wall of flame. Skirnir said to Freyr, "I am afraid to go there. I have no horse that will ride through flame, nor any weapon that will protect me."

Freyr raised his eyes to the heavens, and the light of Gerd's beauty was reflected in them. "If you will woo and win the giantess in my name," the bright Freyr said passionately, "I will give you my sword. Odin gave it to me long ago, and it can fight by itself if owned by a noble and worthy hero. It is my most precious possession."

"All right," Skirnir agreed, "I will try." Travelling on Freyr's horse that could go through the dark, he flew down to Jotunheim to the grim giant Gymir's house. There were fierce dogs surrounding the house, and a wall of flame, but Gerd, hearing thundering hooves outside the gates, invited Skirnir inside safely. There Freyr's servant offered her eleven golden apples if she would return with him to be Freyr's bride.

"Never," she cried, "will I live in the home of any God!"

Rashly Skirnir offered her Odin's golden ring, Draupnir, but this too she refused, saying that her father had given her more gold than anyone could want.

Skirnir began to despair. He knew that he would not safely pass back through the flames or escape the hounds' slavering jaws unless he could out-bargain Gerd. And so he became angry and threatened the giantess with violent and terrible curses that would haunt her life forever. He said he would sever her head from her neck with his bright sword, that he would slay her father, that he would condemn her to sit on top of an eagle's hill where men and Gods would come to stare in horror at her transparent flesh, while all she would see were the sights beyond the gates of Niflheim. "Rage and longing, fetters and wrath, tears and torment, will be yours," he cried out to the startled Gerd. "With three-headed giants you will dwell, and all the Gods will despise you. I write you a charm, and three runes therewith, that are longing and madness and lust!"

Gerd held her hands over her ears, and her bright eyes widened at the venom in Skirnir's threats. Freyr's servant saw that he had frightened her and pressed his advantage.

Softly now he said, "But what I have written, I can still unwrite—if you will say the word."

Gerd held her hands to her cheeks, and letting a soft sigh pass through her full, shining lips, she said, "Find welcome here, brave servant of the most brilliant god, and take this cup of mead. I never thought I would so love the son of Njord, himself once a Wane."

Skirnir nearly leaped in joy and relief, but he did not show all he felt. Still pressing further he said, "Now when shall I tell my master that you will come to meet him?"

"In nine nights' time I will come to the leafy forest outside of Asgard, and there will agree to be Freyr's bride."

When Skirnir returned and told Freyr the news, the impatient god said, "Long is one night, longer are two; how then shall I bear three?"

Gerd kept her promise and became Freyr's wife, yet the cost was high, for Skirnir kept Freyr's magic sword, and Odin's trusted warrior was weaponless from then on.

As Sleipnir thundered and stumbled over the stony terrain, darkness came again, and the elves still flickered around horse and rider like fireflies. Hermod spoke in soft tones into Sleipnir's ear, urging him forward, assuring him that Freyr's friendly elves would not trip him. But he felt the weight of his task lie heavily on him, for Hermod knew that if he failed to reach Niflheim, and Balder remained with Hel, Odin could not count on Freyr's strength to support him in the last battle.

On the fourth day dawn broke on Midgard so late that in some of the valleys there was only a glow above the horizon where the sun could not climb over the hilltops. Hermod, riding over the valley of the sheep farmers, saw the children hunting the flocks.

In the spring of each year these farmers drove all their flocks into the high valleys to graze, and every autumn the great sheep hunt took place. All the men and boys of the farms of this area climbed into the mountains and rounded up the sheep and their lambs from every cave and nook and crevasse and copse. The sheep, as one herd, were driven down the long valley, where now the grass was no longer fresh and green, and all the farmers came together and sorted out their animals, farm by farm, telling them apart by marks on their ears. The new lambs, of course, stayed with their mothers. The sheep then were either slaughtered for winter food or kept in barns of turf, safe from the winter winds.

The boy was only ten, and though he had been allowed to help drive the sheep up the trail in the spring, this was the first year he had gone high on the mountain for the fall hunt. He had been out since dawn and he had climbed higher than his brothers, wanting to prove that he would make the best shepherd of them all. But now he did not see them, and he was afraid he would be lost, all alone in the hills when the sun went down. Into the valley below its rays did not reach, but on the high hill where the boy stood its feeble warmth comforted him. He looked down the ravine below him, but there was a ridge that now separated him from the others. He knew he should go down, but he had heard the lonely sound of a lost lamb calling and he wanted to find it. He climbed around a boulder, thinking there might be a cave where the lamb had found shelter. As he did, a shadow came between him and the low-lying sun.

He looked up and stared at the strange horse and rider in the sky, galloping across the horizon. The child's favorite riddle was in his head—"Who has ten legs, three eyes, one tail, and rides through the sky?"—but the child knew it was not Odin on Sleipnir's back, for he had seen that rider once before! Terrified, he felt the wind of Hermod's flight cold on his cheeks, and forgetting the lost lamb, he scrambled and clambered back down the steep sides of the ravine into the long, stretching meadow that was gray and crisp beneath his feet. His chest hurt, and tears froze on his cheeks as he raced back to his farm.

There he fell on the ground panting and sobbing. He cried out, "Some stranger rides Odin's horse! The heavens will fall if Sleipnir is stolen."

The boy's father and his brothers looked to the sky, but it was dark now, and Hermod and Sleipnir were already out of sight. They recalled that once before the child had claimed he had seen Sleipnir, and that they had thought he was sick. Once again they wondered. The boy's mother picked him up and held him tight in her arms and said he must never go sheep herding again, that it made him ill. "The air is too thin where he goes so high," she said. "He is still only a baby!"

But the father was worried. Although the work was not done, he went to his neighbors. "Come to the *Thing*," he said at every house, "my boy has seen Odin's horse riding north once more!" The villagers gathered at their regular meeting place, and though the town meeting was usually held the first morning of each week, the men talked all that cold night long of what the boy had seen.

19: JOTUNHEIM A MUSPELLHEIM

*Gunnloth sat on a golden stool
And offered the marvelo[u]
mead;
A harsh reply did Odin gi
To her heroic heart.*

On the fifth day Hermod did not look for the sun, because Jotunheim, the world of the giants, was never penetrated by its light. There was a rumor that if sunlight ever fell on a giant, he would fall dead, but the Gods knew too well there was no truth in that!

As he travelled through this land of the Gods' oldest enemies, Hermod sensed the presence of ghosts of the many giants Thor and Tyr and Odin's other warriors had slain. Beli, whom Freyr had killed with his bare fist after he had given Skirnir his sword; and the stone-headed Hrungnir, whom Thor had shattered. Thrym, who had stolen Thor's hammer, was dead; and so was Skadi's father, Thjazi, the eagle giant who had kidnapped Idun. How many widows and brothers of dead giants were around him now, Hermod wondered, breathing on his back, watching him fly by? Hermod did not know, but he knew that once caught, he would not have strength or magic to defend himself. He would have to rely on his wits and on Sleipnir's speed. He would have to find a trouble-free route through this enemy land, and if confronted with a giant, he would have to use his ability to talk wisely—even cleverly—to come out alive. He thought of Njord's guiding words: 'Listen before you speak; think before you fight. No one wants to die in a strange land.''

Before he had time to think further, he heard the sound of a roaring flood or a rushing river so loud that though he saw no lake or waterfall, he thought he must be drowning! He pulled Sleipnir to a halt by the huge rock entrance of a roofless dwelling, in front of which was a stone vessel as tall as a man's barn. The sound came from behind it. Cautiously Hermod led Sleipnir around the side. A giantess sat on a golden stool, the saltless tears streaming down her cheeks causing a river to run over her legs and past her feet and on along all of the paths inside the gate of her home. Her wails were the sound of the water, and her clothing was drenched with her tears. Sleipnir neighed and thirstily lapped at the river by his hoof.

The giantess looked up at Hermod through watery eyes. "Who are you who stares at my distress?" she demanded. "And what do you want?"

"I am Hermod, Odin's messenger," the god replied. "I was only passing through, and I heard—"

"Odin!" the weeping giantess cried out in rage. "Odin! A curse be on him, the most faithless of all the Gods!"

Hermod drew back in outrage. "How can you speak so irreverently of the All-Father," he exclaimed, "the wisest and fairest of all?"

"Fair!" The giantess spat the word out. But then suddenly the anger disappeared from her face, leaving only a deep, sad loneliness. "Tell me," she said softly, "does his sharp blue eye still flash so bravely? And when he claps his hands, does the sound make all men tremble? Is his voice still resonant, and are his thoughts still so deep that they leave you pondering sleepless all the night?"

"How do you know all these things of the Great Magician?" Hermod asked. "Who are you?"

The giantess began to weep once more, and as she wept she said, "Three nights he stayed here with me, three nights and three shining days, and all the time I thought it was because he loved my voice, my thoughts, my soul. But in the end I found that he stayed only to steal my father's treasure!"

Hermod frowned then, for he suspected the truth. "Who are you?" he asked again, "and what was the treasure he stole?"

"I am Gunnloth, Suttung's daughter," the weeping woman sobbed, "and in this vessel you see beside me was the famous mead of poetry that my father stole from the dwarf who made it. Odin, jealous as the Gods have always been of any treasure a giant could find, turned himself into a snake and bored his way right through a mountain to get to our doorstep. And I was fool enough to give him welcome in my father's home. Oh, how I loved him! How it shames me now to remember! And when he asked on the third morning for just one sip of the magic mead that could make anyone who tasted it able to create the finest and most heroic verse, I was so simpering with affection that I said 'surely help yourself!' In three long swallows the vessel was empty, and," she sniffed, "where your Creator stored that much mead will always be a mystery to me." She shook her head.

"Before I knew what was happening, Odin turned himself into an eagle and was off over the forest and the seas that come between our land and yours." Gunnloth paused and wiped at her eyes ineffectually. "I never did see him again," she sobbed. "And since then I have nothing in my life but Suttung's anger for having been so careless, and an empty vessel by which to weep over my betrayal and my lost love."

Hermod was silent, remembering well the day Odin in eagle's shape had flown toward the gates of Asgard. Heimdall had warned the Gods of his approach and of Suttung in hot pursuit. They had rushed out with pots and containers, and just before Suttung reached Odin, the All-Father in eagle form spat the magic mead into the containers in the courtyard, thus providing the Gods with the mead of poetry, so that any of the Gods could taste it. In his haste, however, Odin had spilled a little on Midgard, so some men, too, gained the talent for creating song and verse.

Hermod felt such compassion for this grieving giantess that he was quite without words. But then she spoke again. "No God has visited me since that day," she said. "What brings you to my door?"

"I am on my way to Niflheim to bargain with Hel for Balder's life," Hermod replied.

Gunnloth nodded thoughtfully. "Balder was good," she said, "and anyone who has loved knows the purity of his heart. Yours is a good errand, and I suppose if I cared about living at all, I would wish you well."

"Thank you," Hermod said, still unable to find a way of taking graceful leave. "I did not know there were any friendly spirits in Jotunheim."

"Not many," Gunnloth replied. And then suddenly she held up her hand for silence and turned her head toward the gate. "Be off," she whispered. "I hear tremors that tell me my father, Suttung, is waking. Hurry! His wrath has never lessened. If he finds you here, you will not survive!"

On a sudden impulse Hermod stood up in his stirrups and kissed the giantess's wet cheek and whispered, "Thank you!" Then he pulled the reins against Sleipnir's neck, turning Odin's horse away from Suttung's gate, and galloped over a dark plain toward a tall and craggy black mountain.

As horse and rider flew toward the pass over the mountain, a most horrendous rolling and crashing made Sleipnir rear in fright, and the sound nearly split Hermod's eardrums. Was the universe exploding? Had Gleipnir, the magic chain that held the Fenris Wolf, suddenly broken? Had Ragnarok come without warning? Had Hermod lost his way and thus lost all chance of rescuing Balder?

He clung to Sleipnir's mane, soothing the animal with soft words that also calmed his own terror. When they came through the pass, they saw below them the great poisoned river, Slith, and on the opposite bank, three giant-boys playing a game of catch with boulders as big as men's houses. Each time a boy missed, the boulder fell to the earth, breaking and shaking the mountains themselves, leaving craters like huge pockmarks on the landscape. With his heart beating frantically, Hermod dismounted and carefully led Sleipnir around the rim of the crater valley, across the vile river, until they were hidden from the game players and on their way once more.

On the sixth day Sleipnir and his weary rider came to Muspellheim, the world of the fire-giants. Surt, often called the Scourge of Branches, tended his furnace in the center of Muspellheim, and the sparks that flew up through cracks in the earth's surface had long ago become stars. As Hermod picked his way among the flames, hurrying onward though the fire licked his legs and made Sleipnir snort in pain, he thought of the sun, which he had not seen since he left Midgard. Wistfully he remembered the two children whose task it was to drive the sun and moon on their appointed paths, and the two snarling wolves the giants had sent to chase them on their way. If he didn't get safely through this fire world, the wolves would catch the children and devour them, the sun, and the moon!

Suddenly Hermod found himself between two pillars of stone facing a fire that rose so high he could not see its end. Over his head was the hand of the giant Surt, holding a bellows as big as an oak tree. The pillars, Hermod realized, were Surt's flameproof boots. Somewhere beyond that furnace was the cool, safe shelter of Myrkwood, the dark forest that surrounded Muspellheim. Hermod had to pass so close by the roaring furnace that the draft nearly sucked him and Sleipnir into the rising flames. Just as he thought they were safely past and under the trees, Hermod heard a bellowing laugh that made the fire crackle and the ground tremble.

"Who are you and what makes you think you can pass by the fires of Surt and not be consumed?"

Sleipnir stopped, and Hermod's voice quavered as he spoke. "I am Odin's messenger, sent to Hel to beg Balder's return."

The giant Surt put his gloved hands on his mammoth hips and said, "Odin is too wise to bargain

20: SVARTALFAHEIM— WHERE THE DARK ELVES LIVE

Odin, I know where thine eye is hidden,
Deep in the wide-famed well of Mimir.

On the seventh day Hermod and Sleipnir, tired but persistent, rode through tunnels and caves, along underground rivers and hot streams that sent clouds of steam around their faces. They were deep inside the earth where the dark elves lived. Never did the light of sun or moon reach these depths, and the rock walls were sometimes hot where Surt's fires had burned close. The dwellers of Svartalfaheim were enemies of the Gods, thieves and mischief-makers, well versed in minor magic, but their power was unseen and their ways were devious. Both Gods and giants had used the elves, sometimes trying to ignore the curses the dark little people swore at them for the unhappy tasks they had been set to do.

In this underside of the world were the elf-keepers of the four poles, Nordi, Sudri, Austri, and Vestri. There was Gandalf, who taught magic, and Vindalf, who knew how to ride the wind, and Althjof, who taught the art of stealing, and many others whom Hermod did not know.

He could not see where he went. Stalactites and stalagmites blocked his passage at every turn. Sometimes the tunnel roof became so low he had to dismount and lead Sleipnir through. Sharp rocks cut and bruised both horse and rider, and Hermod could not hurry along the twisting, turning tunnels. He did not know where he was going! He heard laughter from all sides, around corners, echoing, louder and softer and sometimes mixed with the sound of water in the unseen rivers. In this nightmarish darkness, surrounded by sinister sound, Hermod remembered Balder's dreams and felt suddenly close in spirit to his brother god who had so recently passed this way.

Where was Balder now? Had his journey to Niflheim been swift and painless, or slow, frightening, torturous? Hermod wished his trip were over! Picking his way through the labyrinth, he thought about the things he had learned on the long way through time and felt shaken by his new knowledge, his perceptions of the Gods' betrayals! If the Gods were not heroes, who were the Gods, and who could save the world?

A sharp stone cut his forehead, and he put his hand to his head, crying out with the pain. He felt the blood warm on his fingers. Why was he here? What predetermined chain of events led him to this miserable moment, a rider in a dark and narrow world, unable to see, unable to protect himself?

"Odin," he cried into the darkness, "what terrible bargain with fate did you make so that evil infests us all?" Laughter rose high around him. "How the dark elves laugh at me!"

Suddenly he stopped short, one foot in the air. All was silent. Something had changed. Walls were no longer close around him. He sensed he was in a large space, more frightening even than the hurting narrow tunnel. He blinked and stared ahead, but the dark was a wall, blinding him. Then he looked down. There was something he could barely see, a strange, shapeless, swirling glow below his feet. He strained so hard to see that his eyes ached. It was light emanating from deep within a thick, murky pool, dark colors shifting and swirling like pigmented oil. Hermod's heart pounded, and he felt Sleipnir's nose nuzzle fearfully into his armpit. He knew now where he was. If he had gone one step farther, he and his horse would have plunged into the filthy liquid.

With trembling voice he whispered, "Mimir?"

Again the terrible laughter rose like incense around him.

Hermod spoke to the darkness. "What did Odin see in your well? Why am I here? Why do the dark elves laugh at the Gods?"

For answer again there was only the laughter, but one word came through, and he remembered suddenly that Odin had said the same:

"Reflections."

Hermod leaned over as far as he dared and peered down into the pool. There he saw his own frightened face, Sleipnir's head beside him, and nothing more.

Then he steered the All-Father's eight-legged horse carefully around the edge of the dense pool and knew that before these two long nights were over, he would understand the truth. But would he, who was neither brave nor strong, survive and change the course of evil begun so long ago? Would he ever reach Niflheim? Even the thought of entering the land of the dead seemed preferable to him than this! Once again the passage was narrow and the walls sharp and cruel.

Hermod never knew when the end of the seventh night came, because he and Sleipnir were still turning down the tunnels when he heard the sound of hammer and anvil. Then he knew that he had passed into the eighth world, Nidavellir, the land of the dwarfs.

These masters of the world's rock core lived much like the dark elves, and many men confused them. But Hermod knew that here, behind their doors of stone, were the great forges of the dwarfs. Though once they had been maggots on Ymir's flesh, after Odin had given them the shape of men and consciousness, the dwarfs had become the finest of smiths, creating tools and magic weapons of gold and iron for God and man alike. Hermod thought, as he listened to the rhythmic clang, clang, clang of a smith's hammer, of those treasures made for the Gods by Brokkr, Sindri, and Ivaldi's sons.

He had been so long in darkness that he was nearly blinded by the firelight when he came upon a dwarf sitting by a huge waterfall with his iron in the fire. At first glance Hermod thought the strange little man with the pointed lips and fingers spread flat upon his chest was evil in his fishlike stare. His head was so narrow and his eyes so round and bulging that Hermod sensed a shape other than man's in his bearing. The god reined Sleipnir to a halt.

The dwarf looked at Hermod, turning his head to look first with one eye, then with the other, quite suspiciously. "Who are you and what do you want?" the fishlike dwarf asked.

"I am only passing through," Hermod said, "on

my way to Niflheim to bargain with Hel for Balder's return."

"Hah!" the dwarf laughed, a crisp and bitter sound. "There are too many evil and bloodthirsty hearts on earth for Balder to survive. You will never get him out of Hel's hands."

"Who are you to tell me this?" Hermod asked. "And what is that you are making in your forge?"

"I make nothing in my fire," the dwarf mumbled. "Loki saw to that! But it was my curse that brings you on this dark and troublesome road to hell."

"Just who are you?" Hermod asked.

"Andvari!"

Hermod knew the name instantly and sensed that it was not evil but a deep bitterness that he heard in the dwarf's voice. "How did your curse bring me here?"

"Sit down," Andvari said. "The story is not short. And it will serve you well to rest and learn the truth before you go on to Niflheim to bargain with Hel."

Hermod dismounted and sat on a flat rock by the water. Sleipnir drank thirstily, then moved away from the falls and, carefully folding his eight legs, lay down on the stone floor. Andvari stared into his empty forge, put down his hammer, and began to talk.

*I saw there wading through
rivers wild
Treacherous men, and
murderers too.*

Long, long ago, Andvari told Hermod, Odin and Loki and Hoenir went down from Asgard to explore realms they had not travelled. They came to a waterfall and sat to rest beside it, marveling at the beauty of the cascade, the way the high spray caught the sunlight, shattering its rays into pinpoints of every color. "I have made the world and all creatures in it," Odin said, "but whenever I go forth, I find I do not know everything. I have never seen a sight like this before, though I must have known these falls were here."

"Look!" Hoenir said, pointing to a salmon leaping from the foot of the falls, its pink-silver body as lithe and beautiful as anything he had seen.

"That is what I mean," Odin said smiling proudly. Suddenly an otter appeared in the river, caught the salmon in its mouth as the pretty fish fell back into the stream, and swallowed it in two greedy gulps. The otter looked at the Gods and blinked.

Loki picked up a stone and threw it with true aim at the animal's head, killing it instantly. The Gods went on their way again, Loki carrying his prey over his shoulder.

"Well," said Hoenir sadly, "I am hungry, and I suppose we can eat the beast. But I would rather have gone without dinner and let the salmon live!"

The Gods came to a farm and asked for a night's lodging. "We do have plenty of food," Loki bragged to Hreidmarr, the farmer, showing off the dead otter. "I have killed two with one stone. There is a whole fresh salmon inside. Cut him open and see for yourself."

The farmer was not a good man and was a master at black magic. He nodded at Loki's boasting, instantly recognizing the dead otter as his third son. Before the Gods knew what was in his mind, he called out, "Regin, Fafnir, come bind these villains! They have murdered your brother!"

Hreidmarr's two huge, burly boys appeared from the side of the shed, overpowered the Gods with ease, and tied them to each other so they were quite helpless.

Odin said, "What price will you name for our freedom? I will give you enough gold to set you free from labor all the rest of your life."

The farmer raised his eyebrows. "It isn't easy to put a price on your own son's head," he said cagily.

"Name your price," Odin said.

"If you will fill the otter's skin with purest gold, and cover the outside with gold, too, then I will believe my son's life has been paid for," Hreidmarr said.

Odin agreed. "Untie us now," he commanded. Then he said to Loki, "Go to the dwarf Andvari, and bring me all the gold he possesses. He guards the richest hoard in all of Nidavellir and doles it out, fleck by iny fleck. Hoenir and I will wait for you here. Do not be long, for we must return to Asgard."

Loki flew on his magic shoes to the cave by the waterfall. At first he saw nothing there except the gold that winked and glittered from every rock.

At this point Andvari stopped his story, and Hermod looked around him at the high rock walls by the cave. "Here?" he asked the dwarf.

Andvari nodded, and then continued his tale.

At first Loki did not see me, for I was in the shape of a trout swimming in the pool at the bottom of the falls. But suddenly my fire flared up, and the light must have glittered off my back, for he reached into the pool. Before I could get away, he snatched me out of the water. He knew who I was!

I twisted and flipped and tried to squirm out of his grip, but I could not escape.

"Do not flap so violently, little fish," Loki said, holding me so tightly I thought he would crush me, and he looked deep into my eye. "I know you guard the gold that winks at me from these rock walls. Give it to me for Odin's life, or I will kill you." He gave me an extra hard squeeze.

I would not have given Loki a fleck of gold. But for Odin, who gave me breath and thought, I would do anything. So I went limp in Loki's hands, hoping he would let me go before I died for lack of air. He must have thought I was dead, for he looked at me in a strange, frightened way as he held me now in the open palm of his hand. But then I changed into my regular form, nodded to him quickly, and went into my cave. I gathered all my gold as Odin had asked, put it into two great sacks and gave them to

Loki. All I kept for myself was one small gold ring that I had made. It was a magic ring that could produce others like it. With that ring I would be able to make more gold another day. It did not seem like much to keep.

"Is this all?" Loki asked me when I put the bags in front of him.

"Yes," I said.

He lifted the bags to his shoulders but suddenly looked at my hand suspiciously. "What is that?" he demanded.

"Uh, only a little ring," I said. "It is so small it would mean nothing to Odin."

"Give it to me," Loki commanded. "I must have the ring also."

"Please, no," I begged him. "If you let me keep it, I will be able to go on forging gold treasures. All I need is this one tiny ring. Please!"

"Give it to me," Loki said, "or I will squeeze the breath out of you!"

I knew he could do it, too, and I was bitter. So I said, "Greed like yours should have no reward. Here!" I put the ring in Loki's hand, and then I cursed it. I cursed all the gold he had stolen from me, too, so that he and his kind would regret the way he had treated me, who had done him no harm!

I said, "The dwarf's gold shall be the death of two brothers, and the ring the ruin of whoever possesses it!" But Loki only laughed and slipped my pretty ring on his finger. Then he walked out of my cave without turning back. I knew my curse would follow my gold forever.

Hermod looked around him at the black walls. "What happened then?" he asked.

"What happened then is history that many know," he dwarf said, and continued the story.

Vhen Loki returned to Hreidmarr's farmyard, the ods emptied the bags into the otter's skin and then egan to cover the hairy outside. As they worked,)din noticed the ring on Loki's finger. "I like that ing," he said. Loki gave it to him.

Hoenir and Loki called Hreidmarr when the otter vas covered with gold. "But there is still a bristle howing," the greedy farmer said, "right here beside he left ear."

Odin took Andvari's ring and put it on the bristle, nd Hreidmarr was satisfied. The gods were free to eturn to Asgard. Regin and Fafnir sat looking at heir dead brother, filled and covered with gold. They 'id not mourn him, but each thought of what he vould do with the new riches.

Fafnir said, "Father, you take a full half, and Regin and I will share the other half." The boy eached out to the otter's head.

"Get your hand off that gold!" Hreidmarr roared. 'You will have none of it! All is mine."

Regin and Fafnir were hurt and angry at their ather's greed. In the night they plotted against him, nd before dawn Fafnir drove his sword through his ather's heart while the greedy old man slept.

"Well done," Regin said. "Now we can divide the ;old."

"Why should I share it with you?" Fafnir said. 'It was I who was brave enough to wield my sword. 3e off before I kill you too! I never want to see you gain." Fafnir turned himself into a monstrous dragon vith tongue of fire and breath of poisonous fumes. Ie took the gold-filled otter's skin to a cave, and there he lay down upon it and let no man come near

Regin travelled to another part of the world and learned to be a fine goldsmith. He took a young orphan in to live with him as his foster son, a magnificent lad named Sigurd, who grew tall and strong and fearless. Regin loved Sigurd as his own and gave him many things and taught him all he knew. From the beginning he told Sigurd about the dragon that lay greedily on a great hoard of pure gold in another country, how no man had been brave or strong enough to kill it, and how the beast kept all who lived near in terror.

Regin made Sigurd a magnificent sword, which was so heavy no one else had strength to lift it. The sword was so sharp that when Sigurd held it in the river and let a strand of wool drift against it, the blade cut the wool in two. Then Regin outfitted a ship, and he and Sigurd sailed across the sea to the land where Fafnir the dragon lay on Andvari's cursed gold. Regin told Sigurd to kill the dragon, and Sigurd was not afraid.

Without a qualm the brave boy rode to the mountain and found Fafnir's cave. Sigurd hid and waited a whole day to see the path Fafnir took to crawl away from his hoard and drink at a pool. During the night Sigurd dug a trench across this path and lay down in it. The next morning, when Fafnir crawled down the path over the trench, Sigurd drove his fine sword straight and deep into the dragon's heart.

The dragon leaped high into the air and cried out, "Who has reddened his sword with Fafnir's blood?"

Proudly the boy said, "It is Regin's son, Sigurd!"

Fafnir writhed in anger and pain, and a terrible scream came from his throat like the screeching of a herd of horses in a burning barn. And then his cry became feeble, and finally he lay down and died. Sigurd went to the dragon's cave and found the gold. Seeing the little ring, he thought it pretty and put it on his finger. Then he wiped his sword clean and started down the mountain.

"Wait!" Regin jumped out from behind a yew where he had been hiding. "Where are you going so fast?"

"I am taking my treasure home," Sigurd told his father. "I have killed the dragon. The gold belongs to me!"

"Go slowly," Regin said. "You must know the truth. You have just killed my brother!"

Sigurd stopped and stared at the older man. Then he looked at the dead dragon. "This is brother of no man," he said.

"He was my brother," Regin insisted, "and the gold he guarded was rightfully half mine."

"But it was I who was brave enough to kill him," Sigurd argued. "You merely encouraged me. What am I to you now? Villain or hero?"

"I made the sword that you use," Regin said. "We are both villains and heroes, and we must atone for our deeds."

"A brave heart and a strong arm count more in battle than the weapon," Sigurd said. "What must I do?"

For answer, Regin took his knife and cut the heart out of the dragon, then drank deeply of the blood that flowed from its great artery. He handed the heart to Sigurd and said, "Hold Fafnir's heart to the fire and roast it well. When it is fully cooked, you must eat it. I am tired now, for that red wine is heady, so I will sleep. Do as I say."

Regin lay behind the yew and fell into a deep

173

sleep. Sigurd built a fire, held the dripping heart on
a stick over the flames, and sat to wait while it
cooked. When he thought it might be done, he
touched the hot flesh with his finger and burned himself. He put his finger to his lips, and the instant he
tasted the dragon's blood, he could understand the
language of the birds.

A nuthatch on the tree above him said,

"There sits Sigurd, sprinkled with blood,
And Fafnir's heart he cooks."

Another said:

"There lies Regin, dreaming of plans
To betray the son who trusts him so well."

The first little bird said:

"There sits Sigurd, sprinkled with blood,
Waiting for Regin to wake up and slay him."

The second nuthatch said:

"Wise would Sigurd surely be to kill his betrayer;
Then all of Fafnir's gold would be his alone!"

Shaken to the depth of his soul, Sigurd stood up
slowly and went and stared down at the only father
he had known and loved. Yet he believed the birds
would not lie. Sad, but bold and brave still, he took
the great sword and killed Regin while he slept. Then
once again Sigurd picked up the gold, mounted his
horse and rode off to find the woman he had loved for
a long time and who waited for him in a deep sleep
like death behind a wall of flame.

As he rode away the first nuthatch said:

"There rides Sigurd, knowing not
Of Andvari's curse on the gold.

It shall be the death of two brothers
And the ring the ruin of whoever possesses it."

Sigurd found his lovely Brynhild on the mountaintop. He rode straight through the flames to her side, put the cursed ring on her finger, kissed her lips, and she awoke. The joy of the lovers lasted but a short time, for the curse followed them. Before they could ever marry, they both died violent deaths.

Andvari's story was over, and for a long time after the dwarf stopped talking, Hermod sat in silence. He thought about the curse on the gold, about Andvari's words: "Such greed should have no reward." He remembered the vision in Balder's dream, of brother drinking the heartblood of brother, and he thought of the reflections in Mimir's well. *When Odin peered into the well with one eye, he saw into the empty hearts of men he had created.* Balder alone was innocent, but he could not live in a world where greed and murder—the evil passions—became stronger than the good. If Odin had not been strong enough to control what he had made, would Balder—returning from the dead—be able to wipe out such sins as these?

Sleipnir whinnied and stood up. It was time to move on. Hermod climbed on the great steed's back and said goodbye to Andvari. "If I succeed," the god said, "and pass through your world with Balder by my side, I shall tell Odin all of your story. Although it was your curse that brought me here, I cannot feel anything but compassion for you who have sat so long by an empty forge because of the appetites of men."

22: THE LAND OF THE DEAD

Nine worlds I knew, the ⸺
in the tree
With mighty roots benea⸺
the mold.

—The ⸺

On the ninth day Hermod saw the glittering gold thatching of the Gjoll bridge. He urged Sleipnir forward. He had come this far. There was hope! Just as they came to the middl⸺ of the roaring river, a woman appeared out of th⸺ air, armored, with sword unsheathed. She walked t⸺ the middle of the bridge and blocked their crossing.

"Who are you, and what do you want?" she asked "You have not the pallor of a dead man, and onl⸺ the dead come this way."

"I am Hermod, a God, and I am alive," he an⸺ swered.

"Yesterday five companies of dead soldiers rod⸺ across this bridge, and all their footfalls together thundered no more than yours. What business hav⸺ you in Niflheim?"

"My business is Odin's. I come to find Balder i⸺ Hel's domain. Has the shining god passed this way?"

"Yes," said the maiden, putting away her sword. "Nine days ago Balder crossed this bridge, and he travelled down to the northern gate. You may follow him if you can."

Hermod rode on until he came near Hel's high iron gates. When the howling dog Garm rushed out with jaws wide and breast bleeding, Sleipnir did not rear up, nor was Hermod afraid. They knew that so long as they showed no fear, the beast could not harm them. Hermod dismounted and walked straight through the gates into Niflheim.

Then he stood spellbound.

All of the fears he had suffered on the long, hard journey seemed nothing compared to this moment alone inside Hel's gates. Hermod was not a brave warrior. He had not Thor's strength, nor Tyr's fighting skill. He trembled!

The land of the dead was a gray, gloomy, steam-filled place, neither light nor dark, with shapes that changed and moved but revealed nothing. Shadows and sounds came and went. In the distance a faint light seemed to glow. Hesitantly Odin's messenger took a few steps toward it.

He stopped. He heard a scratching sound nearby, and a river running. "Beware the well Hvergelmir," Odin had warned him, "and the serpent Nidhogg, who lies on the corpse-covered bank!" Hermod dared not step farther, but peered anxiously into the half-light. While he hesitated so fearfully, Nidhogg gnawed away at the tree of life, sapping its strength.

Summoning his courage, listening anxiously for sound or whisper that might guide him safely clear of the well, Hermod started toward the light once more. Behind him Sleipnir whinnied uncomfortably.

The light grew stronger, and Hermod could distinguish a roofed shelter surrounded by steps and pillars. Inside he could see clearly now the shape of Hel's throne, where a figure was seated. He stumbled, falling on the steps, and when he stood up and walked past the first pillar, an icy wind made him shiver and froze his quivering lips. Then he remembered all of the dread things about the hag who was Loki's daughter. Her threshold was Pit of Stumbling; her hall was called Sleetcold; her servant was Idler; her kitchen-maid's name was Sloven; Hel's dish was Hunger, and her knife was Famine; Disease was her bed, but Balefire her bedclothes.

Hermod walked to Hel's throne, where she waited for him. The smell of rotting flesh was all around him, and the dirt on the floor was sticky to his feet. Hermod had known what Hel looked like, but the sight of her shrunken flesh—half white so that every bone and vein showed through, and half the blue-black of painfully bruised skin—held him aghast. She did not speak, nor did he, but as he stared in horror, she studied him from heavy-lidded yellow eyes.

Suddenly he realized that the light of her room came from Balder, who sat on a tall stool right next to the hag herself! He was still dressed all in white, as shining and beautiful in death as he had been in life.

"Balder!" Hermod cried out with joy. He opened his arms and would have hugged him had not a bony, sharp-nailed hand of the keeper of the dead gripped his shoulder, holding him back.

"Who are you, and what business have you in my domain?" Those words pierced to the core of poor Hermod's brain, yet the hag's voice made no sound. Just as in dreams sounds are heard in silence, Hel's scrawny lips moved, the sound occurred in Hermod's head, his ears itched with the vibrations of her voice, yet there was no sound in the air between them.

Shaking, he replied, "I come from Odin and Frigga to ask that you let Balder return to Asgard."

Hel raised an eyebrow and turned to Balder, who simply smiled gently at Hermod, but said nothing. He did not look at Hel. Then she turned back to Hermod. Again, when she spoke there was no sound in the air, but he felt hard words inside his head.

"I like having your Balder with me," she said. "He cheers me and brightens my rooms. Why should I give him back to the Gods?"

Hermod cried out, "All the world mourns Balder! And all good things in the world will die if you keep him here." He searched for the right words. He turned to his brother, whose face was so placid, so still, though now there was no smile, just two tears in the corners of his eyes. "Tell her, Balder," Hermod said. "Tell Hel what love is yours in earth and heaven! Tell her you want to go back to Asgard, that spring will not come without you there! Men's children forget their sheep in the mountains, and lambs are left to starve. The buds on the tall trees are already rotting, and the baby swans are dying in their nests."

Balder opened his hands and shook his head helplessly. Hermod looked at Hel, and she said, "He can't speak to you. Only the quick can talk out loud. I am the only one in Niflheim whose words are heard by the living! Now, is it true what you say? Do all creatures mourn Balder?"

"Oh, yes," Hermod said quickly. "Everyone everywhere weeps for him. Oh, do let him ride back with me. All the world will rejoice, and spring will come again if Balder can be alive. The Gods will pay any price you have."

Hel shrugged her blue-black shoulder. "I'll think it over," she said. "Stay the night." Hel pointed to a circle of dead moss by the rotted trunk of a dead tree, and Hermod stumbled down the steps of the woman's room and sank to the ground. Where she took Balder that long night he did not know, for the light was gone from the place.

The ninth night was long and cold, and even in Niflheim Hermod could hear the rumblings of storms over Midgard and winds blowing out of the north. Balder in death had been as beautiful as Balder in life, but time would not always have it so. The moanings of the sick and dying came to Hermod's ears like damp clouds surrounding and threatening him. He did not sleep, and all the long hours he tried not to give up hope.

In the morning Hermod found Hel and Balder side by side just as they had been the night before.

Hel said, "Did you sleep well with my company? They are all sound sleepers."

"I did not sleep," Hermod said. "May I take Balder away?"

"You have told me everyone weeps for Balder," the hag said slowly. "If all things everywhere weep for Balder, the strong and the weak, the quick and the dead, if they all weep for his return, I will let him go. But if there is one creature, one thing, no matter how large or how small, who refuses to shed a tear for your Shining God, then Balder the Good will stay by my side forever."

Hermod cried out for joy. "Oh, climb on Sleipnir's back and ride through the nine worlds home to Asgard, Balder, for I can say truly that all things weep for you!" Hermod reached for Balder's arm, but once again he felt the stabbing grip of the hag's hand on his shoulder.

"Wait," she said. "Balder may not go with you now. He will stay here until I have proof. Now, you messenger of Odin, blood brother of my father, go back to your Gods and Goddesses and tell them what bargain Hel has offered!"

With hope in his determined heart, Hermod walked back to the high gates of Niflheim. There he paused, for he knew by the light that Balder was near. The gods met and for a moment clung to each other. Hermod whispered that it would not be long before Balder was home. Balder, still unable to utter a word, gave Hermod the gold ring Draupnir, which Odin had put into his hand the day of his death. Hermod said, "I will give this to Odin so that he will know I have seen you."

Balder nodded and smiled. Then Hermod went out through the gates, mounted Sleipnir, waved good-bye to Balder, and flew from the north out over the frozen mountains, across the rivers and seas back to Asgard.

*And one night old fights
    Odin's son.
His hands he shall wash no...
His hair he shall comb not,
Till the slayer of Balder he
    brings to the flame.*

High on the golden hillside the massive walls of Valhalla stood a somber guardian, its pitched roof a silver streak in the low sunlight. It seemed to the Gods that the sun did not move during the days and nights Hermod was gone, as if time were stopped and the sun waited for news of Balder's fate.

The rainbow bridge stretched serene, but Heimdall paced it nervously, grinding his golden teeth together. Barely had he seen Hermod a hundred miles off than Sleipnir galloped across the bridge, eight legs flying, nearly knocking him over. Without stopping, horse and rider raced to Odin's courtyard. There all the Gods gathered around Hermod as he dismounted.

Odin came down from his tower, his eye dark blue and soft with unexpressed hope. "Did you find your way to the gates of Niflheim?" he asked.

"Yes," Hermod said. "I passed over the Gjoll bridge, and Garm bellowed harmlessly. I spoke with Hel herself."

The Gods and Goddesses were astonished, and repeated to each other what Hermod said, some with disbelief.

Odin said, "No live man or God has ever crossed that bridge and returned."

Hermod, sensing that Odin doubted his words, handed him the ring Draupnir.

The All-Father looked at Draupnir and then held the ring up so that everyone could see Hermod's message came straight from Hel.

"What did the keeper of the dead say?" the Great Creator asked in a low voice. Frigga came close to Odin and put her cheek to his broad shoulder. Everyone held his breath. The courtyard was silent.

Hermod let his words fall slowly, like the tolling of bells. "If all things will truly weep for Balder, everything everywhere, the quick and the dead, then Balder may return to Asgard. But if there be one who will not weep, no matter how large or how small, alive or dead, then Balder will remain with Hel forever in the land of the dead and forgotten."

As if the clouds themselves had heard, rain fell on Asgard. The Gods and Goddesses began to weep, and so did the heroes and the valkyries, servants and masters. The horses in the stables and wild in the meadows wept; and the dogs and all of the animals in the forests of Asgard wept for Balder. Freyja's cats cried, and the great boar Saehrimnir cried. Even the mighty Odin found that his one flashing eye could shed a tear.

Then Frigga said, "It is not enough that all of us here are weeping. There are other worlds and a thousand creatures in a thousand places who must weep."

And Hermod said, "Yes, every creature and all the elements too must weep, for that is what Hel demands."

Odin clapped his hands and called his messengers, his ravens, his wolves. "Go," he commanded, "go now into all kingdoms and all worlds. Go to the Rime-giants and the hill-giants. Go into the greatest mansions and the darkest caves. Go to the meanest huts and the smallest crab-holes, the coldest snow-banks and the hottest plains, the highest waterfalls and the deepest ponds. Find all creatures living and dead and ask that they weep for Balder. Speak to the leaves on all the trees; speak to the rocks and the pebbles on every beach. In the meadows where the sun still shines, tell the blades of grass, the ferns and the flowers, the lichens and the mosses, how all will wilt and all will die if even one should not weep for Balder.

"Tell the spiders in their webs, and the crabs on the beaches, tell the porpoises and the starfish, the herring and the trout. Tell the gulls and the ptarmigans, the eagles and the falcons, the ponies and the sheep and the goats and the cows. Tell the earthworms who loosen the soil, and the shrimp that flock in icy harbors. All whom I have created shall weep now for my son Balder, that he may return to Asgard, that the good world will not end."

Odin's ambassadors went with tears in their eyes, with his message on their lips from Asgard to all the realms.

After they had gone, Odin turned to the heroes and Gods who stood near him awaiting his orders. "Bring Balder's ship Hringhorn down to the shore; there we will make it ready for the balefire."

Immediately twenty strong heroes laid down their spears and went to get the beautiful ship. They carried Hringhorn on their shoulders and set it on the dry sand by the sea. It was the most beautiful of ships, with twenty-two ribs and as many long, slender timbers bent to form the graceful hull. The prow reached high in a proud S-curve, and the carvings along the keelson were rich and delicate. Only a master craftsman could have built such a ship, for there was no imperfection in design or proportion or structure or decoration.

Odin ordered Balder's servants and many other valkyries to bring Balder's possessions down to the ship. The long procession began, as one by one Balder's treasures were carried from his home high on the hill down the long path to Hringhorn by the sea. From Breidablik they brought his woodcarving tools and his axes, his ship's hardware and the furniture he had made. They carried Balder's jewels and his clothing, beautiful tapestries that Nanna had woven for him illustrating tales of the virtuous Gods and men in the morning of time. All these were placed carefully in the long-bellied hull of Hringhorn. In the center of the ship a bed of straw was made. The Gods stood silently weeping, while Bragi, tears running from his eyes into his long, thick beard, lovingly placed Balder's body, rigid in death, on the gentle straw.

The poet said, "Balder lived in every child's pure heart, and as he grew older, so he came to know and hear worldly thoughts, and with each impure image that came to his consciousness, so a little bit of our Balder died. Let all of us hope he has not died this time forever."

The keeper of the stables came from the barn, leading Balder's beautiful white stallion. There by the sea he slit the brave animal's throat, and as the blood flowed out of him, so did life. It had always been so that a horse would not survive his master.

Two strong heroes carried the carcass up the ladder and placed it in the hull of Balder's ship.

Balder's son, Forseti, came down to the shore carrying Balder's sword. He climbed into Hringhorn's hull and placed the gleaming weapon alongside his father's body. Then he stood up, tears in his eyes, and said, "It was a good sword, but he would never use it. Now his home is as empty of traces of his life as our hearts will be when the balefire consumes him."

All day long the procession went on. People of many races and from many lands came to the shore to see the beautiful ship in which Balder's body lay. Freyr rode down on his shining boar, and Freyja drove by with her cats. Heimdall rode to the shore on his horse, Goldtop, to say his last goodbye, and Vidar and Ull waited silently on the sand. Njord and Skadi and all the Gods and Wanes and Goddesses came by. Hugin and Munin flew back and forth over the ship, keeping count of the mourners and the mourned. Some giants came, tears in their eyes for Balder, and even some dwarfs and dark elves crept into the light of the waning day. All who came still wept and hoped that their tears could prove to Hel that Balder belonged in Asgard. But the Gods who stood and waited and watched the endless procession felt the cold wind blow down from the northern ice, and were afraid that the long, dark winter they knew approached would be everlasting—the dreaded Fimbul winter.

Frigga did not leave the scene. Once she said to Odin, "Where are the messengers?" And he pointed to the first arrivals, his ravens who had travelled farthest and fastest. "What did they find?" she asked him anxiously.

"Everywhere there is weeping," he said.

"Good," said Frigga, and pulled her shawl close.

One by one the other messengers returned. All things, they reported, were weeping for Balder. Rain fell everywhere, they said. All the earth wept. The trees and men and animals, insects and birds, fish and fowl. Even the rocks and metals were wet with tears, just as these things weep when they come out of frost into heat.

"There is still hope," Bragi whispered to Idun.

"There is still hope," Njord said to Freyja.

Nevertheless, Odin ordered that the wood for the fires be gathered and stacked beneath the well-carved hull.

"Where is Hoder?" Frigga said. "He should be here to greet the messengers and hear the news. We may yet have saved Balder! Is there anyone who has not returned?"

Bragi nodded and Odin frowned. "There is one still out," the All-Father said. "An old hero, but faithful, and one who will persist no matter how difficult the task. He has served me long and well, and I sent him to the farthest end of the world."

Frigga looked anxiously at the sun, which hovered on the edge of the sea, turning both the water and the sky crimson. Then Odin climbed the ladder alongside Hringhorn and stepped over the gunwale into the good ship. Once again he took off his own treasured ring, Draupnir, which Hermod had brought back from the ninth world, and once again he placed it in his dead son's palm. Then he went to the prow of the ship and stood up on the gunwale, searching with his long-seeing eye over all the worlds for the last messenger. Hugin and Munin flew to him and stood on either shoulder. A cloud rolled over the water and seemed to bite a dark piece out of the sun's red orb.

Odin clapped his hands and called for the fires to be kindled.

Suddenly all heads turned away from where Odin stood, for an eerie song came across the strand from the west, a high, thin wail like the voice of a lonely bird in flight. The Goddess Rind appeared over the dune, and the horizontal rays of the sun seemed to turn her long black hair to gold. As she moved slowly down the long path, her mournful song flowing from her throat, the Gods could see she carried a great burden in her arms. It was the blind god Hoder, limp and lifeless, and his chest was wet with her tears.

The gentle Njord walked toward Rind. He took Hoder's hand and lifted it to his lips. "What happened?" he asked. Rind told the Gods of Hoder's end.

"Hoder stayed with me last night," she said, "and all of the day before. He said he could not enter Balder's home now that his own soul was stained with such a crime, so I welcomed him." The goddess stopped, and without constraint the mournful melody broke once again from her throat, as if the story she had to tell was too painful to relate without music.

She told how Hoder had sat without moving, his hands in his lap, his blind eyes closed, while everyone around him prepared for Balder's funeral. "He neither spoke nor moved, and so after a time I almost forgot he was there," Rind said.

"Last night I gave birth to a new son of Odin." The goddess went on with her story. "We named him Vali, this infant conceived in the hour of grief and born of our last hope. I was tired, and laid the sweet baby to sleep in his crib, and he grabbed a jewel from my gown and clutched it tightly in his tiny fist. Then I closed the door and left him, and went to where Hoder sat, so silent and motionless as if he waited for death.

" 'Hoder,' I said, 'you have a new brother!' His face broke into a smile for an instant, as if he himself had been reborn, and then he retreated once again to his stony posture. I rested in silence nearby."

The beautiful goddess's voice rose in melody again, and there was not one on the shore who did not turn his ear and still the beating of his own heart to hear her song and story. "Before the night was over, my newborn son of the Great God Odin cried out in his sleep. Hoder, perhaps without thinking, went to the dark room where the baby lay. He put his head close over the infant, feeling with his seeing hands the baby's silken form. But Vali's fist, still clutching tight the sharp-cut jewel, flailed about and struck Hoder's temple—a chancy blow, but lethal. Hoder fell dead on the nursery floor, my son, not one day old, his murderer!"

Odin, who had been listening to the tale of his blind son's death, thought now of the Vala's words, spoken to him in the mists by Hel's gate not so long ago.

"His hands he shall wash not, his hair he shall comb not,
   Till the slayer of Balder he brings to the flame."

Bragi took Hoder's body from the weeping goddess's arms and climbed the tall ladder. He laid the blind god to final rest in Hringhorn's hull.

191

24: THOK'S CAVE

*What maidens are they wh[...]
then will weep
And toss to the sky the yar[...]
of the sails?*

Balder's funeral ship was ready. Breidablik was empty. The mourners, Gods and Goddesses, heroes and valkyries, stood on the shore and waited for Odin's last words.

Odin sent Hugin and Munin forth to look for the last messenger. Then he said quietly, "Light the fires. Bank them, but do not fan them yet. When the messenger returns, there will be time."

"And time to put them out," Frigga said. If the messenger's word was good, they could quench the fire and Balder would return from the dead. But if he failed, Hringhorn would go up in flames, and Balder's balefire would burn.

Everyone's eyes followed the ravens until they disappeared from view. Then everyone watched the unhappy young hero who, hating his task, touched a long smouldering taper to the kindling under Hringhorn's hull.

In the farthest corner of the world, in a desolate dark, damp cave on the side of a high cliff where no man or God would want to be, where solace was impossible and love an unnatural, unknown thing, an old giantess sat and listened to the crashing surf below her. There the Midgard serpent lashed its tail, and now and then a spray of venomous water spewed high into the air. He was anxious to escape his cold, wet exile, and Thok, the giantess, had told him his chance was near.

The last messenger came to the door of the cave and stood looking at the grotesque creature huddled there. For a moment he could not speak. Her skin was dry and yellow like parchment, and her hair was a tangle of tiny snakes with darting tongues and staring green eyes. She was uglier than Hel herself, the messenger thought. He was a gentle hero, who had long ago fought his last battle, but who had learned much about bravery from being one of Odin's chosen favorites.

At first the giantess did not see him, and he listened to the surf and the crashing of the serpent's tail. In a lull he heard the angry cry of a wolf in pain.

Finally summoning his courage, he said, "Who are you, and where have I come?"

The old witch was surprised to see him there. She said, "You are at the end of the earth, after which there is no more, and no man comes here. I am Thok." She ran her knotty fingers through the slithering snakes on her head. "Who are you, and what do you want?"

The messenger said, "I was looking for the last

193

place on earth, and the last person. I have come from the All-Father, Odin, the Mighty One-Eyed Creator."

The hag said, "What does Odin want from me? I have no business with Gods." The wolf howled again, and the messenger turned his head toward the sound. "That is only Fenrir," Thok said. "He is impatient, for he knows he may soon be free."

"Oh, no," the messenger said quickly. "That is why I am here. Odin asks that everyone weep for Balder the Good, for he is in Niflheim with Hel, where the innocent do not belong!"

Thok frowned and pushed a snake off her brow. She tugged at her pointed chin, put her sharp-nailed finger into her ear, and then she said, "I? Weep? These eyes which have seen nothing but the walls of this cave and the empty vapor beyond? Do you think tears could come to them?"

"Oh, yes, I am sure you could find tears in your eyes," the messenger answered her. "You have seen me, and I'm sure others have come to visit you."

"Never!" Thok said sharply. "No one comes here. Why should anyone travel to the end of the world to see me?"

"I did," the messenger said softly. Though he was not brave, he had loved Balder well, and would not leave this miserable creature until he had made her cry.

Thok said, "Tell me more about Balder and why he is in Hel's land, if he is alive and so innocent as you say."

The messenger smiled as well as he could through his tears and began to tell the giantess the long, sad story of Balder's death and Hermod's bargain. He did not notice the two black birds hovering in the air outside the cave, for he was too busy weaving a tale, struggling for the poetic way to tell his story so that the heart of this misery-loving, lonely creature at the end of the earth would be moved to tears.

On the beach in Asgard all the Gods and Goddesses waited for the last messenger to return and for Hugin and Munin to fly back and perch on Odin's shoulders. The tears of the world had flowed so freely that it seemed the whole universe was flooded. In Midgard men and women listened to the rain and heard the sounds of storms all about them. They, too, wept as they huddled in their houses away from the rising seas and the swelling rivers.

Odin, climbing down from the prow of the funeral ship, clapped his hands and called out, "Roll Hringhorn into the sea!" Ten strong heroes ran to the stern of the heavily laden vessel and put their shoulders against the curved sides. All together they pushed and pushed, but the ship did not move. The smouldering fires steamed and smoked, and the smell of charcoal was in the air.

In Thok's dry cave the messenger came to the end of his story. Searching her ugly face for signs of sadness, for a touch of compassion, for a whisper, a flicker of emotion that would tell him his story had reached her heart, he paused. The giantess licked her twisted lips and said, "I'm thirsty."

Pleading with her now, the messenger said, "Did you not find Balder's death sad? Isn't there in your heart just one beat of sympathy for those who loved him, and for the world?"

Thok shrugged. "What is it to me if the world

ends? I am already at the end of it and have always been."

"If I could see one tear in each of your eyes," he said, "if I could return to Odin and tell him that truly the giantess Thok at the end of the earth has shed two tears for our beloved god Balder, then the world will go on and on, life will not end, spring will come next year, all evil creatures will stay bound, and I promise you that this cave will no longer be the end of the world but the beginning of a new world begun!"

Thok scratched her chin and listened for a moment to the howling wolf. Then she said dryly, "How do you know that I am not one of the evil ones? That I would not like to see Loki and his children go free?" She looked out to sea. "There go Odin's ravens. They will tell your All-Father the truth."

In Asgard on the beach the Gods saw Hugin and Munin return. The ravens settled on Odin's shoulders and whispered in his ears.

Odin said with a heavy voice, "Call the giantess Hyrrokkin. She will be stronger than our heroes; she will be able to push Hringhorn into the sea. If she cannot do it, then Balder will live." He sent an eagle off to find Hyrrokkin.

The giantess came striding over the ridge from the east, her bulk filling the whole hillside. She put her hulking shoulder against Hringhorn's hull. All the Gods held their breath. The ship moved. Frigga gasped as if in pain. The rollers burst into flame.

Nanna, seeing the fire leap up along the long curved timbers of Balder's tomb, cried out in a high wail and then fell lifeless on the sand. Thor strode to her side, gently picked up her frail lovely body, and

carried her onto the great ship. Although it was already on fire and in motion, he placed Nanna by Balder's side on his bed of straw. Then Thor came down and joined the other Gods as the fire spread and the ship moved slowly toward the sea.

In the desolate cave at the end of the world the dry-eyed Thok said bitterly to Odin's last messenger:

> "Thok will weep
> With *dry* tears
> For Balder's burial;
> Neither in life nor in death
> Gave he me gladness.
> Let Hel keep what she has!"

All of the Gods and Goddesses, heroes and valkyries, watched Hringhorn roll flaming out to sea. All over the world the light of Balder's balefire turned the sky and oceans red, until the last timber and all that the ship contained were reduced to gray ash.

25: RAGNAROK

Now Garm howls loud before Gnipahellir
The fetters will burst and the wolf run free ...
And in Fensalir does Frigga weep sore!

Three cocks crowed. In the forest near Jotunheim the bright red rooster Fjalar stood on the tallest spruce tree and screamed to the giants to rise in battle against the Gods.

In the western woods outside of Asgard, the cock named Gollinkambi crowed high and shrill, calling the heroes to arms.

On the highest spike of the gate of Niflheim a rust-red bird that had no name opened its beak and roused the dead from their sleep.

The last battle began, and never had there been such a one in all of time. From every corner of the world heroes and giants challenged, fought, and slew each other. Underground rivers turned red with blood as the dwarfs and dark elves were lured from their caves by the thunder and the trembling of the rocks. These dwellers of the inner earth came into the light and fought each other, fought men and animals. No living creature was without his antagonist. The cries of the dying rose like smoke into the air and enveloped the earth. The weeping of women could be heard like water everywhere.

Balder was dead. While he lived, men held to hope, set their sights high, fought and worked and strived for ways to live in peace and goodness. With his death, control vanished, the balance of nature was destroyed, and every evil passion and force was unleashed.

Brother fell upon brother as old jealousies were revived. Men who had suspected their wives or sisters or neighbors of wrongdoing now let their fear and anger rise. Grudge fights, feuds, and duels were fought, but there were no victories. Those who had for years contained their thirst for gold, for power, for blood, now let greed overcome them. Armies marched without leaders. Ships' crews mutinied. Looters swarmed over the land. No man trusted his neighbor, nor fathers their sons, nor kings their subjects. No man's sword was clean of blood, as heart after heart was pierced. The whole world sounded of violence and smelled of death. Even the valley of the shepherds was invaded by fighting hordes, wolves, and men. Children were orphaned and wounded and killed. Women were widowed and murdered. Sheep were left by the wolves on rocky hillsides to bleed and die.

Odin stood in his watchtower hearing all, seeing all, knowing and fearing what was still to come. Frigga, covering first her eyes, then her ears, pleaded with him to ride out on Sleipnir where all could see him.

"Go, go!" she cried. "You can stop the bloodshed! Only you!" But Odin did not speak, nor did he move.

He stood straight and still while the walls of Valhalla shook with the sounds of fury in the worlds below. In the morning of time, he remembered, after the war with the Wanes had ended, he had stood in the mists outside of Niflheim and heard the Vala's words.

"Brothers shall fight and fell each other,
Sisters' sons shall kinship stain.
Hard it is on earth with mighty sinning,
Axe-time, sword-time, shields are sundered,
Wind-time, wolf-time, ere the world falls;
Nor ever shall men each other spare!"

From the east a thrashing wind rose as the tawny eagle-giant, Hraesvelgr, spread his mammoth wings and took flight. As he circled up and up, gales blew from all directions so hard that trees were torn from the soil by their roots. Farmers and their huts and their herds were tossed like hailstones across the land into the pounding sea.

Heimdall, hearing the cock crow and the blasts of war on earth, raised his Gjaller-horn to his lips and blew three mournful tones. All the high Gods came to the bridge, met and talked and braced themselves against the winds that tore at them.

"What shall we do?" Thor asked Odin, shouting above the wind. "Where shall we hold our ground?"

"There is no stopping the holocaust now," Odin replied.

"Go to the well once more," Njord cried to the All-Father. "See what the keeper of your other eye will say to you now. Mimir may still have a glimpse of wisdom that he has been hiding from you."

"Yes, go," Tyr said. "We will fight to the death, but . . ."

"I will go," Odin said.

The Great Creator stood below the root of the world ash, Yggdrasil, and looked into the pool. He waited for the murky waters to clear and for the old sage to appear. Hraesvelgr flew on, and Odin felt the tree of life shiver and shake. As he stood there, her great limbs that reached into heaven, chewed tender by the deer, split and bent and broke off one by one

Odin stood among the falling branches and felt beneath his two great feet how the gnarled root gnawed to weakness by the dragon Nidhogg, shifted and groaned and broke loose from the soil. Rivers that flowed from the springs beneath the roots ran together as a raging flood, carrying huge boulders ice chunks as big as mountains, along in the turbulent waters. Odin wondered at how long Yggdrasil had stood so tall, appearing straight and strong, when in truth she had been eaten away to a hollow shell.

During all the generations of his life, while he had appeared straight and strong, all-wise, all-powerful, had he too been hollow and weak? Yggdrasil had been the vision of strength for the elements, just as he had been the vision of strength and purpose for men. The water cleared for a moment, and he looked down deep; there—just as it had been in Balder's dream—he saw his *own* eye staring up at him, and at the bottom of the pool was the sun.

Odin did not wait to see or hear more. He flew back to Asgard where his Goddesses, his warriors, his loyal and loving family, waited for their leader.

The old ash vibrated like a plucked string. Ratatosk, the poor squirrel, ran terrified from top to bottom and back again the topmost branch that was left. A gust of wild wind snatched him screaming from the branch, and then the rotten old trunk split vide, splintered, and fell with a deafening crash that was heard throughout the cosmos.

The earth heaved up, and fire belched forth from Surt's furnaces, sending molten rock miles into the air. High cliffs crumbled; mile-deep cracks opened wide, and mountains broke apart. From far off to the north Odin heard the baying of Garm, Hel's bloody hound. Two wolf-sons of Fenrir ran from the arms of their giantess mother, and one swallowed the sun and the other the moon. All the earth was in sudden darkness.

Odin put his golden helmet on his head and took up his magic spear, Gungnir, which could find any mark. Then he called to his highest Gods, his strongest warriors, his best giant-killers, who were Thor and Tyr, Freyr and Ull and Vidar. "Come stand with me now," he said. "We must be ready for the last battle." Hiding his true thoughts, he said firmly, "We have overcome the giants before. We will again!" Thor pulled on his gauntlets, tightened his belt, and gripped Mjollnir. Ull tightened his bowstring and packed his arrows. Vidar laced his boots high, and Tyr sharpened his sword.

To each of his Gods Odin assigned a company of heroes. Then he called his armor-clad valkyries, and some he told to guard the gates of Asgard; some he assigned to protect the Goddesses and the mansions of heaven; some he called to the battlefield to care for the fallen soldiers. He called to Freyja to lead her army of heroes, and ordered Freyr's wife, Gerd, to raise her shining arm and light the world of the Gods so they might be ready for the onslaught.

Then Odin went to Heimdall and told him to look well at all horizons. "When you glimpse the invaders, blow your horn again, and then join us on the battlefield." Then the Highest-of-All led his great army to the dark Plain of Ida, outside the walls of Asgard, where they waited for the gathering giant forces.

On flew the wind-giant, Hraesvelgr, over the waves that tawny eagle catching and gnawing at men's corpses as he swept along. The terrible ship, Naglfar, made of dead men's nails, broke loose its moorings and carried the giants to battle, the huge giant Hrym with shield held high, at its helm. Naglfar rose on tidal wave that flooded over the land, carrying in its briny torrent the unconquered Midgard serpent, son of Loki, spewing venom and poison breath over the countryside. Its wildy lashing tail destroyed whatever was in its path.

Across the black and angry sea from the north came another ship, this one straight from the land of the dead. It was Hel's ship, with all her wild and bloodthirsty champions on board, eager to avenge themselves on God and hero. Who, but Loki—his irons having melted—stood at the helm of the dark ship, his blue-black daughter, Hel, on one side of him, and Thok, the giantess from the end of the world, on the other, urging him on. There was a wildfire light in Loki's eyes, and his chin was high. The snakes his hair had become told all whom they passed that Thok was his mother by another name.

In the bottom of Hel's ship was the whole army of fire-giants, with Surt, the Scourge of Branches, at their head.

Around and around the elements flew, fire and water and wind. The Gods stood fast, shoulder to shoulder on the Plain of Ida as the storm raged

round them; and the Goddesses clung to one another
n Frigga's home, Fensalir, where they wept and
prayed.

Both dread ships appeared out of the black sky at
the end of the rainbow bridge at the same moment.
Heimdall raised his Gjaller-horn to his lips, but before
his breath could push out the warning sound, Loki
leaped from the prow of Hel's ship, threw the horn
over the bridge, and was wrestling with the far-
sighted watchman of the Gods.

The guardian of heaven and the evil blood-brother
of Odin grappled in a life-and-death struggle on the
rainbow bridge between earth and heaven. Loki's
fingers reached for Heimdall's throat, and Heimdall
held Loki's shoulders, driving his knee hard into the
wild god-betrayer's chest. Silently, desperately, the
bitter struggle went on, with first the Gods' guardian
on top, and then the Gods' betrayer. The two could
neither gain on each other nor loosen their holds,
and they fought until breathless, suspended between
heaven and earth. Each spent all the strength that
he had, until in one sudden instant, both hearts failed;
and Loki and Heimdall fell dead.

The two ships moved on, Naglfar and Hel's vessel.
Bifrost trembled, swayed, and like a great cloud
blown to nothing by the high winds, the rainbow
bridge split apart and disintegrated until there were
only tracers of color in the air where it had been.
The challengers from Niflheim and the sons of Muspellheim surged forward, Surt leading the way, his
flames now lighting the battleground and the skies
as high as Thjazi's eyes.

The Gods and heroes stood on the Plain of Ida,
boldly unafraid of the onrushing giants. Odin took

the center column, Thor stood ground on one side
Tyr and his company on the other. Freyr and Vida
led the second columns. Odin met Hrym, and thei
swords clashed. Giants and heroes began to fall. Ty
swung with his good right arm, and Thor's hamme
flew again and again. The field was strewn wit
giants' heads and maimed heroes, but now no magi
raised the fallen. Bragi and Njord stood, swords i
hand, at the edge of the field, watching their love
ones fight.

Suddenly there was a lull. There were no mor
giants, but only the leaders left—Surt stood alone
fearful and flaming. The high Gods paused, awe
before his hot brilliance. There were no heroes now
Suddenly Bragi called, "Look out!"

From behind Surt's fires the bloody hound Garn
raced out, his jaws open and his fangs bared. The
dog leaped at Tyr's throat, but the god fended hir
off, catching the jaw in his one good hand, throwin
Garm to the ground, where he held him under hi
boot. Odin and Thor held Surt at bay while Tyr an
the dog fought on. Finally Tyr managed to clam
his big hand around the animal's throat, in a deat
grip. But as the dog fell limp, it sank its fangs dee
into Tyr's wrist, and blood rushed out of the grea
artery. Tyr died slowly, for the valkyries were unabl
to stop the flow. Sadly Odin and Thor and the other
fought on.

Suddenly there was a shout from the high plac
where Hermod stood: "Look out!" A crashing o
stones and a clanking of chains shook the ground
and from behind the giants' ships the Fenris Wol
charged into the clearing. He stopped suddenly
looked to one side of the field, and then the other

His eyes were red and his great mouth open, dripping, showing his mammoth teeth. His lips were curled in an angry snarl. He shifted his weight from side to side as he searched the battlefield.

"It must be Tyr he looks for," Bragi said trembling. Just then the wolf saw his betrayer dead, and Garm beside him. The wolf opened wide his jaw and cried to the universe. "I am robbed of my revenge," he howled, and his lower lip dragged the earth while his upper touched the sky. Then he narrowed his red eyes, turned toward Odin, and slowly stalked the Highest-of-All.

Odin planted his feet wide and held his magic spear, Gungnir, straight before him. The menacing son of Loki approached. Silent Vidar stood on one side of Odin, and mighty Thor on the other. Freyr waited just behind. They all knew that one of them alone could not grapple with the monster and win.

The gods stepped forward toward the wolf. Fenrir's tongue dripped heavily out of his mouth. Thor raised his hammer and took careful aim. Odin raised his spear.

The wolf moved closer. Just then with a wild snarling roar the Midgard serpent writhed and twisted onto the battlefield, heading straight for Thor. The earth shook, and the air was hot as the serpent whipped his venomous tongue. Thor threw his hammer and grabbed two of the serpent's arms, trying to wrestle it away from the other Gods who were left, and away from Odin. God and beast tangled and wrestled and twisted in a terrible struggle. Freyr tried to come to Thor's aid, but he had no sword with which to strike! Long ago he had given it to Skirnir, and this was no giant—like Beli—whom he could kill with his bare hands.

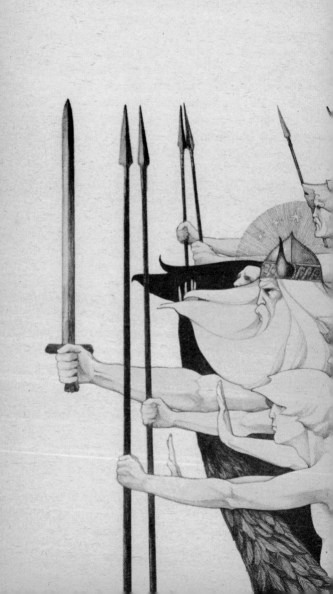

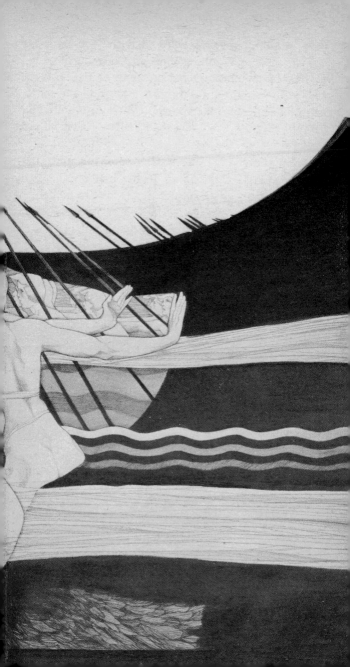

A blinding flash went out, and the fire-giant Surt leaped on Freyr, killing him with one burning blow to his head. Fenrir moved closer to Odin. Odin held his spear straight ahead of him; Thor and the serpent wrestled. Silent Vidar and the Ull tried to help Thor, but the serpent's tail lashed so violently that all they could do was stay out of its path. Finally in a tremendous burst of strength Thor took the spiny neck and twisted it three times in his hands. The scaly killer of men and Gods fell dead, but as he fell, he breathed upon the face of the son of Jord and Odin. The great god Thor raised his gloved hands to his eyes, walked nine staggering steps, and fell to the ground.

Fenrir growled lustily, and Odin, flanked now by Vidar, Ull, and Forseti, stepped bravely toward the beast. Ull let one of his arrows fly. The wolf reared in pain, opened his jaws, and before Gungnir could leave Odin's hand, the beast swallowed the Great One-Eyed God.

Surt's flaming weapon downed Ull and swept Bragi and Njord and Hoenir who were in his fiery path. But Vidar rushed at the wolf, and lifting his huge, heavy-soled boot, rammed it down the throat of the god-destroyer, then plunged Odin's sword into Fenrir's heart.

"Odin, Father-of-All, your death is avenged," the silent Vidar cried. But Surt's hand felled him too, and all who were left in heaven and earth.

Then it happened as the Vala had said:

"The sun turns black, earth sinks in the sea,
    The hot stars down from heaven are whirled;
Fierce grows the steam, the life-feeding flame,
    Till fire leaps high about heaven itself."

The earth turned around, but the sun did not rise. The Fimbul winter began. For full three years all the world lay in darkness. The northern ice moved down, slowly, over the burned-out, crusted land, crushing everything in its path.

26: AFTER
THE STORM

*Now do I see the earth anew
Rise all green from the wave
again.*

—The V

Outside the gates of hell there was, in another time, an old grave, and damp mists swirled about it. One-eyed Odin had stood at that desolate place and called forth a long-dead wise woman who was buried there. He had used charms and magic words that made her unwillingly travel the long road up from her death to where he stood.

He had asked her many questions about the past and future of the world that he had made, for he loved his lands of men and Gods, and he loved all of his children, and he knew that they were threatened.

The old wise woman was angry at Odin for making her come along that cold road up from the dead, and when she spoke, she told him more than he wanted to know. She told Odin that the world he had made, and all things in it, would be destroyed.

And so it was.

She also spoke of a new world that would rise out

of the ashes of the crushed, dead one, but Odin did not live to see it. Those of his children who were reborn in the morning of the new time were not Gods—all-powerful—as he had created them, but more like men with memories. They sat and talked of other days and of the Gods who once had lived in a land called Asgard and dined each night in a hall of heroes called Valhalla. . . .

The boy woke suddenly and rubbed the sleep from his eyes. It was light, and he looked about for his lost sheep. Then he panicked. He stood up and searched all around him. He shut his eyes again, opened them now so wide they hurt. He could not see one familiar scene, object, house, stone, or tree!

He did not know where he was!

How long had he been asleep? He ran his hands down his arms, feeling unfamiliar cloth. Then he touched his hands together, feeling his own flesh as if he did not know what it was like.

He was bewildered, alone in a landscape so strange that he did not even know who he was! Slowly now he scanned the ground around him, studying first the gray rock ledge where he stood, then the lip of the glacier twenty feet below, from which tiny rivulets of icy water ran. Then he looked farther away. Black mountaintops seemed to touch the gray sky. For craggy miles there was no stirring of air, no sound nor breath except his own. All was cold, colorless, and dead. Gray hills seemed to lean against the mountains, and below the hills great gray slag plains stretched wide, worn to tired flatness where the glacier had been. Now he heard the sound of it, creaking and groaning, rumbling down below him. He knew where it went, but he did not know how he knew. Beyond the cliff's edge was the sea.

He heard a sudden sharp scream and wheeled. From the mountaintop an eagle rose, circling slowly, flying over the descending valley. The boy was frightened as the eagle flew toward him, and he saw great menacing talons spread open and a yawning hungry beak. The big bird went past the rock where the boy stood, and over the cliff. Then it dropped out of sight. The bird rose up a moment later with a large fish in its mouth.

The boy smiled in relief, and then felt a pain in his stomach. He was hungry! He looked at the rubble around him. Where in this bleak, dead desert would he ever find something to eat? He climbed down from the rock and began to walk along the side of the glacier toward the lowland and the sea.

As he picked his way among the boulders and clambered across crevasses in the valley, a sense of excitement seemed to fill the air. He realized that the sound of water running, which at first had been just a distant trickle, was now everywhere around him. The light was changing. Rocks began to glisten; colors appeared and changed with each passing second; pink and blue and yellow were everywhere. As he came around a tall, erratic pillar of porous black stone, a tremendous scene appeared before him. A waterfall— which seconds before had been a tall ladder of ice— burst into motion and cascaded down the valley. The spray flew high into the air from the rocky floor, and each droplet of water caught and held the first rays of sunlight that had come across this land in three long years. The Fimbul winter had ended.

The boy heard the torrential falls and saw the rainbow-strewn mist and felt the sun's warm hand

on his neck, all in one magic, overwhelming moment. He stopped, held his hands to his cheeks, closed his eyes in wondrous disbelief. When he opened them, he saw beside him a blueberry bush full grown and ripe with fruit. He was standing in fresh green grass, and his bare feet were wet, for every blade was laden and shimmering with dew. He ran his finger along a slender green leaf, collecting the fresh water, and touched his lips. He picked five blueberries and ate them. He turned his head to the sky, which was bright blue and shining. Glittering on top of a puffed cloud was a castle, finely jeweled and delicately wrought with gold, and the sunlight shone through.

The boy laughed out loud, suddenly remembering. His laughter reached up to the highest peak, where the satisfied eagle sat. It reached down to the deepest hollow, to a quiet pool where a family of trout awakened. His laughter rang from the rocky hillsides, and it rolled over the ocean waves. The music travelled around the whole new world and out of it until the sound reached the sky.

Balder reached the gate first. He opened it and let his brothers enter into their new home. Just as Gimle's golden door swung wide, the reborn gods heard distant music. Balder the Good, Hoder the Blind, Vali the Brave, turned and looked down where they saw green grass growing. In the dewy meadow below they saw the first child of the race of men who would inhabit the new world. They heard his laughter, and they were glad.

AFTERWORD

The Norse myths, on which this book is based, were first written down by poets in Iceland between 900 and 1200 A.D. They are contained in two books, *The Elder,* or *Poetic Edda,* and *The Younger,* or *Prose Edda.* We can expand our enjoyment and understanding of these myths if we know a little about that isolated island in the North Atlantic Ocean, one thousand miles from Europe and two thousand miles from America.

Iceland is a land that actually burst forth from the sea. It was formed by volcanoes which spewed layer upon layer of lava, creating high mountains in the ocean. Iceland's mountains are the northernmost peaks of a volcanic ridge that runs all the way up and down the middle of the Atlantic Ocean. During the fifty million years since its birth, the mountains have been eroded by wind, rain, and glaciers. What is left in the center of the island are snow- and ice-covered mountains and plateaus of basalt, the rock formed when lava cools and hardens quickly. Iceland's shores were shaped as the molten lava flowe down to the sea. It is a tortured, twisted landscap of fire and ice, with startling peaks and cliffed valley cut by the tremendous power of underground to rents, huge waterfalls, glaciers, volcanoes, and th turbulent sea. Yet the treeless flatland that rings th mountainous lava desert is good velvet-green farn land.

The rough seas that surround Iceland, whos northern shore just touches the Arctic Circle, do nc freeze even in winter, because the Gulf Stream flow around the island, warming it. (Greenland, in cor trast, whose southern tip is far south of Iceland, is frozen waste because it is surrounded by the icy Lat rador Current from the polar seas.) In winter, how ever, great chunks of polar ice break loose and floa about Iceland's northern shore, blocking the wate ways and making seagoing hazardous, if not impos sible.

On Iceland the winds are strong and the storm sudden and violent, but the climate is temperate– warmer in winter than New York City. The sun mers are balmy, but of course short because of th latitude. Although the sun does not actually sta above the horizon for twenty-four hours in midsun mer, it dips so little below that it is said a man ca read without artificial light at midnight. The lon summer days and bright nights permit good farmin of barley and wheat, but the short season make many other food crops impossible. Icelandic childre have known for centuries where in the mountains t collect mosses and lichens, (those simplest of plan forms) which they use for both food and fuel.

To the inhabitants of Iceland, the hot turbulenc of the earth's molten center is always sensed if nc seen, for some of the volcanoes still boil and erupt. The island is laced with underground rivers and springs, many of which run hot, and at intervals enough pressure builds up to send steaming fountains high into the air. The largest of these, which spouts a column of steam two hundred feet high, was named "Geysir" by early inhabitants, and the word has come into our language to mean all such geysers including "Old Faithful" in Yellowstone National Park. Almost every home in Reykjavik, the largest city in Iceland, is heated by water piped directly into the houses from hot underground rivers that are tapped one to two thousand feet down in the earth. Icelandic children can swim year-round in outdoor pools filled with water from the hot springs.

The original Icelanders came mostly from Norway, but some came from Norse settlements on the Faroe and Orkney islands, Scotland, England, and other North Atlantic island groups. The first Norsemen who settled on Iceland discovered a small colony of Celtic monks from Ireland, which they quickly conquered and which merged with the new population. Throughout all of Iceland's history there was travel back and forth across the Atlantic to Scandinavia and the English islands, so that Icelandic blood is quite mixed.

Today there are 200,000 Icelanders, of whom about 6,000 are fishermen. Twenty percent of the population is engaged in the fish-processing industry, for the banks off the coast are nearly always thick with herring and cod. Many Icelanders are farmers who raise sheep, goats, cows, and ponies. In the past fifty years, and particularly since the advent of air travel, a number of industries have developed, among them textiles, cement, fertilizers, chemicals, and leather goods. There are no mineral resources on Iceland, for lava and sand are poor providers, and there are no trees, so that fuel has always been a problem. Until recently nearly all houses were made of turf because wood had to be imported.

Poets and writers count strongly among the people of Iceland today, just as they did in earlier days. There are books in every farm and city home; there is one hundred percent literacy, and all education is free. The Norsemen who stayed and raised their families on this isolated and largely uninhabitable volcanic island turned to reading and writing—perhaps because a thousand miles of cold and treacherous ocean separated them from the nearest land in any direction. It was the Icelandic poets who wrote down and thus preserved the great Norse sagas and myths in poetry and story.

The tales told in the Eddas, the oldest Icelandic books, seem to have two parallel themes. The first is an attempt to explain and understand the elements of nature, which in Iceland are so commonly violent (or evil), like the giant who sits disguised as an eagle at the end of heaven and creates wind on earth by beating his wings. When he is angry, there is a gale. Even the characteristics of the landscape itself have their mythological parallels. Norway, the land of the past, has great old forests; Asgard, the land of the Gods, is surrounded by forests. Yet Iceland, the land of the present—like Midgard, the land of men—is treeless and has been since the great Ice Age. The slender and sparse birch groves that existed when the first settlers came did not survive excessive cutting. It does appear that the heaven these rugged men imagined for themselves was, in some respects, similar to their memory of a more beautiful former homeland. Indeed, it is part of Ragnarok, the cataclysmic destruction of Odin's world, that all the trees are torn off the land of men. It is interesting that in spite of the importance of serpents of the sea in these stories, there are no snakes or reptiles on Iceland.

The second theme of the Eddas is an attempt to understand and explain the ways of men who acted with regular violence, just as their ancestors in Norway did. Among the Norsemen the practice of manslaughter was frequent and popular, although there were laws against it. However, occasionally someone slaughtered too many men at one time, or for poor reasons, or killed a man whose grieving friends were powerful. Then such a murderer was punished.

A Norwegian named Thorvald Asvaldsson evidently killed too unscrupulously even for his time, and was exiled. He settled with his family on the northernmost peninsula on Iceland, a point overlooking the Arctic seas. A number of years later, in 982 A.D., his redheaded son Eric followed in his father's tradition and killed two men. Eric the Red was sent into exile from Iceland for three years. During that time he sailed west and came to a shore that was nothing but ice and rock, inhospitable and rugged. For the years of his exile he explored this new land, and then returned to Iceland with tales of his discovery. He called this land Green Land, for he said "it would make men's minds long to be there" if he gave it an attractive name. He was so convincing that when he returned to Greenland he was followed by four or five hundred people on fourteen ships that also carried cattle, horses, sheep, goats, chickens, dogs, and household goods. It was from this colony, less than twenty years later, that Eric's son Leif continued the explorations of the seas to the west, and discovered, settled, and explored North America, which was then called Vinland.

Although the Icelanders did continue the Norse, or Viking, tradition of brawling and killing for some time, as has been told in the Sagas, they were to become the first republic in the New World and probably one of the most peace-loving and peace-preserving nations in the world. Today there is no military force in Iceland; and there is even a law against the sport of boxing.

The Eddas are a loosely connected group of poems and stories about the origins of the world, about Odin and the Gods and men he created, and about the elements of nature in the form of giants. The oldest written works are by sundry unknown poets and were collected into one document by a poet named Saemond. This book is called *The Poetic Edda, The Elder Edda,* or sometimes *Saemond's Edda.* The exact date of the writing of *The Poetic Edda* is unknown, falling somewhere between 800 A.D., when Iceland was first settled, and 1200 A.D. Then a poet and historian named Snorre Sturluson wrote a more or less continuous tale that was called *The Younger Edda,* or *The Prose Edda.* Snorre Sturluson quoted heavily from *The Poetic Edda* and seems to have based most of his book on it, but he also includes some stories and details about the Gods that do not apear in the earlier book. The language of the original is Icelandic, which is to the other languages of Scandinavia—Danish, Swedish, and Norwegian—as Latin is to French, Italian, and Spanish. These two books have been translated, studied, and recreated in whole or in part by poets, writers, and scholars from then until now.

GLOSSARY

Because the stories in the Eddas were created over many centuries by word of mouth before they were ever written down, and because they traveled with their raconteurs over the northern world, there are many conflicting names as well as facts and fantasies relating to the Gods. The several scholars who have translated these poems from the original old Norse manuscripts have attempted to codify and identify names accurately, but they, too, often differ.

It may help the reader to become familiar with Icelandic inflections (and Scandinavian in general) by studying the following rules. The strong accent is always on the first syllable, indicated by ′. When there is a second, weaker accent it is indicated by ″. The syllables often contain the final consonant, as in *Fran′ ang,* or *Frigg′ a.* The consonant *d* is interchangeable with *th* so that *Odin* can also be spelled *Othin.* The guide to pronunciation below is approximate.

VOWELS AND CONSONANTS THAT DIFFER FROM ENGLISH

oe—pronounced like the German ö or the *eu* in the French *peut*

ae—
ei— } pronounced like the ā in *fame*

i—pronounced like the ĭ in *in;* sometimes like the e in *her*

o—pronounced like the German ö

g—pronounced like the *g* in *go*

hv—pronounced like the *wh* in *what*

hr, hl, hn—add a breathy sound before each consonant

j—pronounced like the *y* in *young*

BELI (Bel′ ee) A giant whom Freyr killed with his bare hands. 154, 209

BERGELMIR (Bear′ gel·mir) The only giant to escape drowning in the rivers of blood that flowed from the dying Ymir's veins; the ancestor of all giants. 24, 26, 46

BESTLA (Best′ la) Odin's mother; Borr's wife; known as "the gentle Bestla." 23

BIFROST (Bif′ rost) The rainbow bridge between Asgard and Midgard. 26, 37, 77, 87, 88, 89, 105, 112, 141, 182, 207

BILSKIRNIR (Bil′ skirn·ir) Thor's mansion in Asgard; it had 540 rooms. 74, 112

BLOODY-BREASTED HOUND See Garm.

BORR (Bohr) The first good giant; Odin's father; Bestla's husband; Buri's son. 23, 25, 26, 27

BRAGI (Brah′ gi) A god; Idun's husband; the wise poet and story teller. 12, 15, 16, 22, 24–25, 26, 29, 32, 35, 49, 51, 72, 73, 88, 92, 93, 102, 103, 105, 106, 107, 108, 110, 121, 123, 124, 129, 136, 185, 189, 191, 208, 209, 210

BREIDABLIK (Brayd′ a·blik) Balder's mansion in Asgard "which nothing unclean could enter." 36, 88, 135, 185, 192

BRISING NECKLACE (Bris′ ing) The goddess Freyja's most precious possession, a jeweled necklace made by the Brising dwarfs. 75, 77, 80, 82

BROKKR (Brockr) A dwarf; the goldsmith Sindri's brother. At Loki's request Brokkr brought magic gifts of gold to the court of the Gods. 113–17, 121, 164

BRYNHILD (Brin′ hild) Warrior woman whom Sigurd loved and awakened with his kiss. "Bryn" = coat of mail; "hild" = warrior. 175

BURI (Boor′ i) Odin's grandfather; Borr's father. 23

CHAOS The time before the morning of time, before the world was created, when there was nothing but fire and ice and a steaming void between. 24, 145

COSMOS The time of the ordered worlds as Odin created them. 24, 145

FJALAR (Fiahl′ ahr) The red rooster whose crowing awakened the giants and called them to the last battle. 199

FOLKVANG (Folk′ vahng) Freyja's dwelling in Asgard. 75, 88

FORSETI (For′ set·i) A god; Balder's son; god of justice. 15, 74, 88, 107, 109, 132, 133, 188, 210

FRANANG'S FALLS (Frahn′ ahng) A waterfall where Loki, disguised as a salmon, was finally caught. 131

FREKI (Frek′ i) "Greedy"—One of Odin's wolves, who sat by his place in Valhalla and ate his share of meat. 13, 15 *See also* Geri.

FREYJA (Fray′ a) Goddess of love who shed golden tears; the owner of the Brising necklace; Njord's daughter; Freyr's sister; Freyja drove a chariot drawn by two cats. 14, 15, 38, 39, 75, 77, 78, 79, 80, 81, 88, 92, 139, 183, 188, 189, 203

FREYR (Frair) The bright god; Njord's son; Freyja's brother; husband of the giantess Gerd; keeper of Alfheim. 15, 17, 22, 77, 115, 116, 123, 124, 128, 131, 132, 133, 135, 139, 148, 149–51, 154, 188, 203, 208, 209, 210

FREYR'S BOAR *See* Fearful-Tusk.

FRIGGA (Frig′ a) The highest goddess; Odin's wife; mother of Balder and Hoder; Frigga wore a shawl of hawk feathers. 11, 12, 16, 19, 26, 29, 35, 36, 38, 46, 47, 51, 71, 72, 73, 74, 87, 88–93, 94, 95, 96, 98, 99, 106, 107, 109, 117, 118, 119, 120, 121, 123, 127, 128, 129, 138, 146, 179, 183, 188–89, 192, 196, 200, 207

GANDALF (Gahn′ dahlf) A dark elf. 161

GARM The bloody-breasted hound that guarded the gates of Niflheim. 41, 128, 177, 182, 203, 208

GEIRROD (Gayr′ rod) The fire-giant, whom Thor killed. 73

GERD (Gehrd) A giantess; Freyr's wife; her arm was so bright it could light both earth and sky. 149–51, 203

GERI (Gehr′ i) "Ravenous"—One of Odin's two hungry wolves who sat by his place in Valhalla and ate his share of meat. 13, 15 *See also* Freki.

GEYSIR 219

GIMLE (Gim′ lay) The new hall of the Gods in the time of Rejuvenation. 216

GINNUNGAGAP (Gin′ nung·a·gahp″) The steaming void between fire and ice in the time of Chaos. 20

GJALLAR-HORN (Giahl′ lahr·horn″) A golden horn, which Heimdall blew to warn the Gods of approaching danger. 87, 90, 201, 207

GJOLL BRIDGE (Giohl) The bridge over the Gjoll River, which flowed outside the land of the dead. 128, 176

GJOLL RIVER See Gjoll Bridge.

GLADSHEIM (Glahds′ hame) Odin's hall in Asgard where the highest gods met in council. 36, 38, 49, 103

GLEIPNIR (Glayp′ nir) The magic chain with which the Gods bound the Fenris Wolf; it was made of the sound of a cat's step, the spittle of birds, the breath of fishes, the roots of mountains, the nerves of bears, and the beards of women. 49, 50, 92, 158

GLITNIR (Glit′ nir) Forseti's home in Asgard with roof of silver and pillars of gold.

GNA A lesser goddess; Frigga's maidservant. 94, 95, 96

GNIPAHELLIR (Gnip′ a·hel″ lir) A cave at the edge of the land of the dead.

GOLDTOP Heimdall's horse. 188

GOLLINKAMBI (Gol′ lin·kahmb″ i) "Golden comb"—The cock who wakened the heroes and Gods to the last battle. 199

GOLLVEIG (Gol′ vayg) "Mighty gold"—A Wane woman who was kidnapped by the gods and thrice burned. 145–46

GREENLAND 218, 221

GUNGNIR (Goong′ nir) Odin's spear, a gift of Ivaldi's sons; it could find any mark and always returned to the hand of the owner. 113, 203, 209, 210

GUNNLOTH (Goon′ loth) A giantess; Suttung's daughter; guardian of the mead of poetry. 156–58

GYMIR (Gim′ ir) A giant; Gerd's father; he surrounded his home with a wall of flame. 150

HEIDRUN (Hayd′ run) A goat that stood on the roof of Valhalla. His udders kept the Gods supplied with mead. 14

HEIMDALL (Hame′ dahl) A god, watchman of Asgard; guardian of the rainbow bridge. He could see one hundred miles and hear the grass grow. 47, 87–89, 105, 106, 141, 157, 182, 188, 201, 203, 207

HEL A hag; Loki's daughter by the giantess Angrboda; Odin gave Hel the land of the dead—Niflheim—for her domain. 41, 46, 86, 90, 111, 127, 128, 137, 138, 144, 147, 151, 157, 159, 160, 166, 176, 177, 178–81, 182, 183, 188, 191, 193, 194, 198, 203, 206, 207

HEL'S SHIP One of two that carried the giants to the final battle. 206, 207

HERMOD (Hair′ mode) The fleet-footed god; Odin's messenger. 24, 77, 128, 129, 135, 137–39, 141, 142–45, 147, 148–49, 151–53, 154–60, 161–66, 167, 169, 170, 175, 176–81, 182–83, 189, 194, 208

HEROES Men who died bravely in battle and who were carried to Valhalla by the Valkyries; Odin's soldiers; also called "fallen heroes," and "chosen heroes." 11, 13, 14, 15, 20, 73, 86, 87, 88, 93, 98, 103, 109, 122, 124, 127, 128, 132, 146, 183, 184, 188, 189, 192, 193, 195, 196, 198, 199, 203, 207, 208

HODER (Hod′ er) The blind god; Balder's brother; second son of Frigga and Odin. 15, 16, 18, 19, 20, 27–28, 29, 35–36, 43, 46, 51, 88, 90, 91, 92, 109, 110, 122, 123, 124, 126, 128, 129, 136, 144, 189, 190–91, 216

HOENIR (Hon′ ir) The timid god; Odin's companion on trips. He was given as hostage to the Wanes in exchange for Njord, but he soon returned to live among the Gods in Asgard. 36, 47, 100, 101, 103, 127, 147, 167, 168, 169, 171, 210

HOFVARPNIR (Hawf′ vahrp•neer) "Hoof-tosser"—Frigga and Gna's horse which could ride over land and water. 94, 96

HRAESVELGR (Rays′ velgr) The wind giant; a huge eagle who sat at the corner of heaven. When he flapped his wings the wind blew on earth. 18, 22, 30, 203, 206, 220

HREIDMARR (Rayd′ mahr) A farmer, father of Regin, Fafnir, and of the otter that Loki killed. 168, 171

HRINGHORN (Ring′ horn) Balder's ship. 184–85, 188, 189, 191, 192, 193, 195, 196, 198

HRUNGNIR (Roong′ nir) A giant; his head and his heart were of stone, as well as his shield and weapon. 154

HRYM (Rim) A giant; helmsman of the ship, Naglfar, which was made of dead men's nails. 206, 208

HUGI (Hoog′ i) "Thought"—Utgard-Loki's servant who raced against Thor's servant boy, Thjalfi. 64, 69

HUGIN (Hoog′ in) "Thought"—One of Odin's ravens. 13, 110, 117, 188, 189, 192, 195, 196. See also Munin.

HVERGELMIR (Wher′ gel•mir) The spring in Niflheim, beneath Yggdrasil's root, in which serpents lived and from which many rivers flowed. 30, 128, 177

HYMIR (Him′ ir) A frost-giant who went fishing with Thor, and whose wife had many heads. 82–86

HYRROKKIN (Hir′ rock•kin) The giantess whom Odin called upon to push Balder's ship into the sea. 196

ICELAND 217–22

IDA FIELD, or The Plain of Ida (Ee′ da) The field in Asgard where the Gods met and where battles were fought. 206, 207

IDUN (Ee′ dun) A goddess; Bragi's wife; keeper of the golden apples of eternal youth. 16, 32, 78, 88, 92, 102, 103–09, 119, 121, 154, 189

IVALDI'S SONS (Ee′ vahl•di) Dwarfs who were fine gold-smiths; they made Sif's golden hair and other gifts for the Gods. 113, 115, 116, 164

JORD (Yord) "Earth"—Thor's mother; Odin's first wife. 62, 210

JORMUNGAND (Yor′ moon•gahnd) See Midgard serpent.

JOTUNHEIM (Yoh′ tun•hame) Land of the giants. "Jotun" =giant; "heim"=home. 30, 51, 53, 65, 66, 68, 78, 80, 81, 102, 149, 150, 154, 157, 199

LAUFEY (Lowf′ ee) A giantess; Loki's mother. 111

LOGI (Lawg′ ee) "Flame"—Utgard-Loki's servant who raced Loki at eating. 63–64, 69

LOKI (Loh′ ki) The wily god, son of the giants Laufey and Farbauti; husband of Sigyn; mischief-maker and evil thinker; parent of the Gods' most dangerous enemies; provider of the Gods' most precious gifts; cleverest magician. 12, 37, 38–39, 47, 48, 53, 54, 56, 57, 59, 62, 63–64, 67, 69, 71, 72, 74, 75, 77–81, 86, 100–08, 110, 111–18, 119–22, 124, 130–35, 138, 166, 167–71, 178, 196, 206, 207, 209

MAGNI (Mahg' ni) Thor's strongest son.

MEAD The foaming ale that the Gods and heroes drank in Valhalla. 14, 43

MEAD OF POETRY 73, 88, 156–57

MIDGARD (Mid' gard) The land of men. 14, 19, 25, 26, 31, 37, 39, 53, 69, 81, 87, 89, 92, 100, 119, 145, 151, 157, 159, 195, 220

MIDGARD SERPENT The serpent son of Loki and the giantess Angrboda. Odin cast it into the sea where it grew so large it encircled the earth, threatening all seafarers; also called Jormungand. 69, 81, 84, 85, 86, 92, 105, 111, 180, 193, 206, 209–10

MIMIR (Mim' ir) A dark elf; keeper of the well of knowledge that lay beneath Yggdrasil's root. 10, 34, 52, 109, 163, 201

MIMIR'S WELL 10, 30, 34, 36, 40, 72, 135, 163, 175, 201, 202

MISTLETOE 96, 118, 120, 122, 123, 124, 126, 127, 138

MJOLLNIR (Miahl' nir) Thor's magic hammer; a gift of the dwarf Brokkr. In Thor's gloved hand it could smash giants, break mountains; it caused thunder as it flew through the air and it always returned to Thor's hand. 35, 53, 57, 58, 59, 65, 68, 73, 74, 75, 77, 78, 79, 80, 81, 84, 85, 109, 114, 116, 117, 154, 203, 208, 209

MODGUD (Mawd' good) The maiden who guarded the Gjoll Bridge outside of the land of the dead.

MUNIN (Moon' in) "Memory"—One of Odin's ravens. 13, 110, 117, 188, 189, 192, 195, 196 See also Hugin.

MUSPELLHEIM (Moo' spell·hame) Land of the fire giants. 100, 158–59, 207

MYRKWOOD (Mirk' wood) The cool forest that surrounded the land of the fire giants. 159

and Mimir's well, 34–35, 72–73, 135–36
and Thjazi's eyes, 100–10

RAGNAROK (Rahg' na•rock) The final conflict between
Gods and giants, when all elements, forces of nature,
and evil rose in battle to destroy men, Gods and all
of life. 10, 44, 46, 135, 144, 158, 199–210, 221

RAINBOW BRIDGE *See* Bifrost.

RATATOSK (Rah' ta•tosk) A squirrel that lived in the
tree of life carrying messages up and down its trunk
from heaven to hell. 30, 202

REGIN (Reg' in) Hreidmarr's son; Fafnir's brother; Sigurd's foster father. 168, 171–74

RIME Vapor out of which the giant Ymir was born. 20,
22, 23

RIME-GIANT Frost- or ice-giant. 184

RIND (Rind) A lesser goddess; mother of Vali. 44, 129,
190–91

ROSKVA (Rosk' va) A little girl who became Thor's servant; Thjalfi's sister. 53, 54, 57, 59, 62, 67

RUNE (Roon) A written message telling the future, or
providing rules by which men should live. 29, 72, 126,
145, 147, 150

SAEHRIMNIR (Say' rim•nir) A boar that the Gods cooked
each night for the feast in Valhalla, and that lived
again each morning. 15, 16, 183

SCANDINAVIA 219

SHIP'S HAVEN *See* Noatun.

SIF A goddess, Thor's wife. Her long hair was made of
pure gold. 15, 47, 73, 78, 88, 93, 106, 112, 113, 115

SIGURD (Sig' oord) A hero, foster son of Regin; a beautiful, brave, and strong man; slayer of Fafnir, the
dragon that guarded Andvari's cursed gold. 172–75

SIGYN (Sig' in) A goddess; Loki's wife. 112, 135

SINDRI (Sin' dri) A dwarf, Brokkr's brother; the fine
goldsmith who made Thor's hammer, Freyr's boar
and Odin's ring. 113, 114, 115, 116, 164

SKADI (Skah' di) A giantess, daughter of Thjazi; Skadi
became Njord's wife, and later the snow goddess.
102, 137, 139–41, 154, 188

THJAZI (Thiahz′ i) A giant; Skadi's father; in eagle's form he kidnapped first Loki, and then the goddess Idun. 100, 102, 103, 107, 108, 109, 110, 117, 119, 139, 140, 154, 207

THOK A hag, witch or giantess of unknown lineage who lived in a cave at the end of the world. 193–96, 198, 206

THOR The mightiest god; first son of Odin and Jord; father of Mothi and Magni; Sif's husband; killer of giants, possessor of Mjollnir, the magic hammer, and of gloves and girdle which gave him great strength. 15, 26, 35, 50, 51, 52–60, 61–70, 71–73, 74, 75, 77–86, 88, 98, 103, 106, 107, 109, 112, 113, 115, 116, 117, 118, 121, 123, 124, 128, 131, 132, 135, 154, 177, 196, 198, 201, 203, 208, 209, 210

THOR'S HAMMER See Mjollnir.

THRIVALDI (Three′ vahl·di) A nine-headed giant. 73

THRYM (Thrim) A frost-giant who stole Thor's hammer. 74, 75, 77, 78–81, 154

THRYMHEIM (Thrim′ hame) The mountaintop home of the giant Thjazi and his daughter, Skadi. 102, 108, 139, 140, 141

TOOTHGIFT In old Scandinavia, a gift to an infant on the occasion of his first tooth. 149

TREE OF LIFE See Yggdrasil.

TYR (Teer) The one-handed god; Odin's bravest soldier; god of war. 15, 26, 35, 47, 48, 49, 50, 72, 88, 92, 96, 98, 107, 123, 132–33, 146, 154, 177, 201, 203, 208, 209

ULL (Ool) A god; Thor's stepson; Sif's son; the archer. 189, 203, 210

URD (Oord) "Past"—A fate, or norn; keeper of the spring beneath Yggdrasil's root where the gods came to refresh themselves. 30, 87, 103

URD'S WELL The spring from which the morning dews came. See Urd.

UTGARD-LOKI (Oot′ gard·loh″ ki) King of all giants; an extraordinary magician. 53, 60, 62–70, 71, 72, 73, 74, 118 See also Skrymir.

VALA (Vahl′ a) The dead wise woman of hell. In order to

235

learn the future, Odin called her up from the grave
9, 10, 41, 43–44, 45, 46, 51, 52, 71, 90, 91, 93, 110
126, 191, 201, 210, 212–13

VALHALLA (Vahl' hahl·la) "Hall of heroes"—The great
dining hall in Asgard where Gods and heroes feaste
each night. 11, 13, 14, 45, 49, 52, 62, 87, 98, 103, 106
118, 120, 129, 145, 182, 201, 213

VALI (Vahl' i) Son of Odin and the goddess Rind; half
brother of Balder and Hoder; avenger of Balder'
death. 44, 190, 216

VALKYRIES (Vahl' ki·ris) "Choosers of the slain"—War
rior women who brought dead heroes from the battle
fields of Midgard up to Valhalla; Odin's servants
14, 73, 93, 183, 185, 192, 198, 203, 208

VANAHEIM (Vahn' a·hame) Land of the Wanes. 141
145, 147

VANIR (Vahn' ir) See Wanes.

VE (Vay) Odin's brother; Borr's son; Ve and Vili helped
Odin create the world and give life to men. 24, 2

VEGTAM (Veg' tahm) Pseudonym for Odin. 43

VESTRI (Vest' ri) "West"—One of four dark elves who
held up the corners of the world. 24, 161 See also
Austri, Sudri, Nordri.

VESTRSALIR (Vestr' sal·ir) "Western Hall"—The goddess
Rind's home in Asgard, where Vali was born and
Hoder died. 44

VIDAR (Veed' ahr) The silent god; slayer of the Fenri
Wolf. 123, 127, 128, 188, 203, 208, 209, 210

VILI (Vee' li) Odin's brother. See Ve.

VINDALF (Vind' ahlf) An elf who knew how to ride the
wind. 161

VOLUSPO (Vohl' us·poh) First poem in the Poetic Edda
the wise woman's prophecy, telling of the creation
and destruction of the world.

WANES A race close to the Gods but not of them or o
men; a semi-celestial group whom men also wor
shipped; dwellers in Vanaheim; also called Vanir
9, 17, 34, 37, 72, 138, 141, 142, 145, 146–47, 151
188, 201

WESTERN HALL Home of the goddess Rind. 129